MARIE SOLEIL

Contents

Prologue

THEA

A year ago, I slapped Ethan Taylor in the face.

For the record, he deserved it.

I had just moved to Canyon Cove, home of the True Trophy Wives of Orange County. Settled beside the ocean in southern California, it was a gorgeous place to start my new life and career as a seamstress and designer.

Unfortunately, my new career needed a little help. So I took a job as a server for a high-end catering company to help pay the bills. It wasn't a terrible job. I actually enjoyed getting to see the drama unfold for Orange County's elite.

But what I didn't enjoy was Ethan Taylor.

Son of Rhonda Taylor, one of the "Trophy Wives," Ethan looked like a Ken doll come to life. And as someone who loved playing with Barbies as a child, I'll admit that he made my heart skip a beat the first time I saw him in person. Handsome, classy, with light brown hair styled to perfection and deep blue eyes that probably made any girl give him whatever he wanted.

But I'm not any girl.

I knew better than to get involved with people who attended these events. I had my fill of them back home in San Diego, and they were only out for themselves. Ethan was no different. He reminded me too much of someone who shall not be named. At least not right now.

The first night I saw him, I was serving an event at the Cove Hotel, holding a tray full of bacon-wrapped shrimp. Everyone was thrilled to see him. He had some magnetic pull that demanded attention. He looked like a model in his suit and held himself with poise and grace.

After a while, Ethan waltzed my way. I had seen him arrive earlier with a stunning tall, blond woman on his arm. But now, he was all alone.

"Hello, gorgeous," he murmured, taking a piece of shrimp from my tray. "I haven't seen you around here before."

I blinked a few times. Was he talking to *me*?

"I would've remembered that red hair anywhere." He started reaching for my signature feature, which was tied into a low bun, but I pulled away from his grasp.

"Feisty," he said with a wink.

Ugh. So disappointing. He was too pretty to have a good personality. What a waste. I turned away from him, looking for someone who wanted the appetizer and wouldn't touch me inappropriately.

I saw him at several events after that night. He always brought a gorgeous date (but never the same girl twice), and he walked around like he owned the room. Maybe he did. His family came from crazy money, and most people worshiped the ground he walked on.

I could always feel his eyes on me. He'd get a sample from my tray, escorted by his blond date of the night, and ask some kind of question that made me feel lesser-than. Where I was from, who my family was, what I did outside of catering events. My answers were short and to the point. I tried to convey that I wasn't interested—come on, his dates were right there!—while still being professional. But my answers seemed to intrigue him more and more. I felt like an animal in the zoo that he couldn't stop watching. Sure, I was flattered, but I didn't want his attention.

On that fateful night, Ethan went too far. He approached me alone this time. Without his date to keep him in check, he tried asking me more questions about my life. I kept replying with one-word answers, but he didn't get the hint.

"What kind of car do you drive?" he asked.

"Honda."

He smirked. "Not the most exciting mode of transportation." He paused, waiting for me to say something else. "I've got my Porsche parked around the back," he continued, pronouncing it *Por-sha*, and slipped his hand around my waist. "Maybe you'd like to come and I can give you a—"

He never got to finish that sentence, because I turned around and used my ballet trained balance to slap him in the face, while still holding on to my tray. Daddy taught me not to let a man mess with me, and I wanted to make him proud.

For the final blow, I leaned in and whispered in his ear, "Don't ever speak to me again." I straightened, turned, and walked away from him.

From then on, Ethan stayed a fair distance away from me. But I always felt his eyes on me.

And I'd be lying if I said I didn't watch him, too.

One

ETHAN

I looked out the window of my office in Park City down to the streets below, heaving a gigantic sigh. At three in the afternoon, I was ready to head home. Not that I had much to enjoy back at home, but at least it wasn't...here.

My father/boss walked down the aisle, his loud voice thundering as he laughed with Scott King, the Golden Child. His newest partner. Not me, his son. You'd think that Nicholas Taylor would want his only son to share the helm at his investment banking firm, but apparently Scott had earned that privilege of right-hand man.

Any outsider observing the two of them would assume Scott was my father's son. Not me, the scrub sitting in a sea of cubicles. In fact, anyone who watched our lives over the last ten years would think the same thing.

I scowled at them as they walked by. Scott turned his head and narrowed his eyes at me. I went back to my work.

Investment bankers always had a million things to do. The hours were long, but at least I had a job.

And it brought in good money.

Couldn't complain about that.

My phone rang in my pocket. Expecting it to be a client, I gathered myself together and took a deep breath, putting on my best front. But a glance at the phone made me genuinely smile.

"Hey, Gran," I said into the phone.

"Ethan, darling, so good to hear your voice," she warbled.

"How's Manhattan treating you?" I asked.

"Hot and muggy. August in New York is unbearable. I need to come visit you in California instead."

I smiled. "Well, I'll be there for our visit soon enough. Is everything ready for your party?"

Every year, Gran threw a benefit to save the giant pandas. Even though they were reclassified as "vulnerable," not "endangered," we didn't dare tell her. She still loved those big bears and wanted to help. Who knows, maybe her benefits had actually helped their status over the last twenty years.

"Not quite. You know how these things are," she said. "There are so many details to consider, and no one ever does them correctly."

"I hear you," I said.

"But enough about me. Who are you bringing as your date?" she asked.

I smoothed the side of my hair, trying to think how to stall the conversation. "I haven't decided yet."

"I don't want one of your floozies, Ethan. You need to be more serious about finding the right woman. Remember last year's girl? I couldn't talk to her for more than five minutes. She had nothing in her brain. You're smarter than that. I don't know why you keep company with girls like that."

I didn't want to tell her I knew who the right woman was. But she had unfortunately slapped me in the face a year ago. There was no way she'd be interested in taking a trip to New York with me any time soon.

"I'm having fun, Gran. You have to respect that."

"No, I don't. You're a grown man. It's time you found someone to make babies with."

I cleared my throat. "That's a bit much."

"I want great-grandbabies. Sue me."

"I never would."

She cackled. "Smart boy." Gran, my mother's mother, had more money than my father would even know what to do with. My parents' marriage was a match made in banking heaven.

And I was set to inherit almost all of it.

I glanced at my father as he entered his office with Scott. "I'm glad someone thinks I'm smart."

"I know you are. You just need to make better choices."

"I try," I mumbled. "I don't think I would recognize a better choice if it was in front of my face."

She paused, and I could imagine her tapping her long, perfectly pink manicured nails on the table that sat next to her overly elaborate sitting chair. "Tell me who she is."

"Who *who* is?"

"The girl. The one you're trying to forget."

Dang. Gran was perceptive. I had to give her points for that. Her mind was sharp. "Her name is Thea."

"Oh, I like that. A Greek goddess, huh?"

"She might as well be. Except she's not Greek. She has red hair and green eyes. But she hates me."

Gran chuckled. "Feisty. I already like her."

"Yeah, me too." I sighed. "She's a dance teacher, but she wants to be a fashion designer."

"You seem to know a lot about her already, even though she doesn't like you." Gran said. "Do I know her family?"

I bounced my leg, feeling extremely uncomfortable with this situation. "No. She doesn't come from money."

"That's not a problem."

"Maybe to you." I glanced around to make sure no one was eavesdropping. "I don't have a problem with it. But I think she hates the whole scene."

"Scene? Are you in a play?"

I stifled a laugh. "No, Gran. The world we live in. Well, *our* world."

"Ah. She thinks we're materialistic."

I shrugged. "She might not be wrong."

Gran hummed. "There's more to you than just money. But you haven't done a good job of showing that to anyone else."

"I don't know about that." Money and appearances were all that mattered to my father. At this point, I wasn't sure if it was a show or my actual personality. All I knew was that I wanted to make my father notice me.

I took in a deep breath. "There's no way she'd agree to come with me."

"I want nothing less. You're bringing Thea."

I laughed out loud. "That's impossible."

"Consider it my party gift. You bring this girl, that's final."

I shook my head. "Oh, Gran. You're crazy."

"Maybe I am. Are you going to deny a dying woman her last wish?"

"You're not dying."

"I could be," she protested.

"You're not."

"You're right. I'm not." She heaved another sigh. "I just want to see you happy."

I looked around the office. Was I happy? Not really. Work was miserable. The hours were long, the job was difficult, and I constantly felt like I came up short to Scott's perfect standards. I knew how his sister, Amy, must have felt growing up.

And when I wasn't at work? Parties, galas, and dates with girls who just wanted to show up on the arm of Ethan Taylor. At the end of the night, I was alone in my apartment, the missing piece of my life leaving an empty hole.

But Thea.

From the moment I saw her, I knew she was special. She was effortlessly gorgeous, in a way that I didn't see often here in Orange County. She didn't dress to impress; her catering uniform was as unflattering as they come. A white button-down shirt, black slacks, her red hair in a low bun. But she carried herself with poise and grace, smiling at everyone.

There was a magnet drawing me to her. I couldn't explain it. But those first few conversations, her witty comebacks and ability to see through my lines, made me want her more than anyone else.

I made a huge mistake hitting on her the way I did. But at the time, I didn't know any other way. Every girl I'd approached in the past was impressed with what I had and could offer them. It had almost become a game for me, seeing how far I could push those girls. It was ridiculous, and I cringed thinking about the way I talked to her. A few weeks later, I went on that one date with Amy Carter (formerly King, aka Scott's sister), and she told me exactly what she thought of me. That changed my outlook. Then Amy gave up everything to live her own life and become her own person, and we were good friends.

But Thea.

She slapped me in the face. And I couldn't get her out of my mind. If I could ask her out all over again, I would.

Could I?

It was worth a shot.

"I've got it!" Gran exclaimed, startling me from my thoughts. "Tell her you need her to be your fake date."

"Fake date?" I repeated. "Like in a rom-com movie?"

"Exactly! It always works. You pretend to date, and she falls for you instead. You can tell her...tell her that your inheritance depends on you bringing a nice girl along."

"First, no one would believe that. And second, Thea would probably say no so that I *couldn't* get my inheritance."

"Hmm," Gran hummed. "I see the dilemma. Then tell her I don't want one of your floozies, and you told me you had the perfect girlfriend named Thea."

I huffed a laugh. My Gran was a little crazy, but I still loved her. "I'll see what I can do."

She squealed. "That's my boy. I'll see you next week."

I smiled from ear to ear. "Sounds good. Bye, Gran."

I hung up the phone and glanced at the clock. It was almost time to leave. I checked the schedule online for The

OC Dance Project, where Thea taught ballet. Maybe I'd done a little internet stalking in my spare time. Don't judge me. If Thea was teaching tonight, I'd have a chance to talk to her. No parties, no serving trays, and, hopefully, no slaps.

For Gran, I had to try.

A flash of brilliance came to me. A memory of what happened every year around Gran's benefit. The perfect way to entice Thea to come along.

I scrolled through the contacts on my phone until I came to the right person. Dialing her number, my heart raced with anticipation.

"Hello, Carmen? I have a favor to ask of you."

Two

THEA

Few things are as satisfying as finishing a sewing project. All the hours spent picking out fabric, cutting meticulously, piecing together, sewing, ironing, gathering, hemming, and finally taking out those last few stray threads are so worth it when you see the final product put together on the hanger.

I took a long look at the pageant gown I had just created for Maritza Sanchez's niece, Cordelia, and admired its beauty. It took more hours than anything else I had worked on, even though it wasn't a "glitz" gown. Still, I wanted my name to be on something I was proud of. Now that the waist had been taken in, the skirt hemmed, and the pink accents added, it was probably my best work.

I surveyed my kitchen, filled with scraps of fabric and threads, and sighed. My least favorite part—cleaning. My tidying skills were better than I had expected for living on my own, but I had to fight against my natural, slobbish tendencies every day.

Just then, my phone alarm went off. Saved by the bell. I'd have to clean after work instead. Darn.

I ran to my dresser and pulled out clothes for teaching dance. Even though I trained mostly in classical ballet, I loved coaching the competitive jazz teams. My job teaching dance only took three hours a week. I split the rest of my time between serving at catering events and sewing custom costumes or dresses. It was a lot to juggle, but it kept me busy. Living alone could be...well, lonely.

I pulled on my leggings and loose top, tied my long red hair into a low side ponytail, blew a kiss to my fish, Gerald, and ran out the door, nearly slipping on a scrap of fabric in the kitchen. Maybe cleaning up was important, after all.

Dashing down the stairs of my apartment building, I leaped into my old, reliable Honda and headed to the studio, The OC Dance Project. Today I was coaching my friend and fellow teacher Ivy's little sister and her elite mini team. Those seven-year-olds gave me a run for my money, but they were incredible dancers and full of energy and life. It was a rewarding job, for sure.

My speakers blared Fall Out Boy's song "Dance, Dance." I had an obsession with emo music from the mid-2000s. Ivy and I shared a mutual love of millennial music, except she loved pop, like Britney Spears and *NSYNC, and I loved rocking out to the emo bands.

A phone call coming through the Bluetooth interrupted my head banging. I smiled as I answered the call. "Hey Mama," I said into the speakerphone.

"Hey, love bug. Driving to work?" Her bright voice filled

my car and squeezed my heart. I missed her. She was only an hour away, back home in San Diego, but sometimes the distance felt further.

"Yep. I have the elite mini dance team right now."

"Sounds fun. And catering tonight?"

"That's right. How did you know?"

She laughed. "You keep yourself very busy. Let me guess, you were sewing until the last minute, too."

I giggled. "You got me."

"I hope your apartment isn't as much of a mess as your bedroom was."

I sighed. "I'm trying." My mom knew me better than anyone, even though I had been gone for over a year now. "But I just finished the pageant dress for Maritza Sanchez's niece."

"The one on True Trophy Wives?"

"Yep! I'm hoping it'll give me some new clients." I babbled on for a few minutes, excitedly telling her about the dress.

"That's great, love bug. I'm so excited for you." She hummed, hesitating for a moment.

I knew she was holding back. "Just say it, Mama," I said.

"I'm thrilled for you. Truly. But I worry about you. Are you having any fun?"

"Of course I am. Sewing is fun. Teaching dance is fun."

"More than that. Something with friends."

Friends? I didn't really have those, but I had to appease Mama somehow. I racked my brain for a minute. "Oh! I went over to Ivy's house to watch her appearance on the Trophy Wives show."

"Thea. That was months ago."

Hmm. She had a point. "Well, I hang out with Ivy other times, too."

"At the studio? Or for fun?"

Another point for Mama. "I think work *is* fun."

"How did I know you'd say that?" She laughed, and my heart warmed. We knew each other so well, and sometimes it hurt being away from her. "I'm glad you enjoy your job. I really am. But you need to enjoy life. Go on a date. Something."

I scoffed. "Date? There's no one good around here."

"You could always come back home," she said in a sing-song voice.

I shook my head even though she couldn't see. "No way. You know I can't."

"I know." She sighed. "I'm proud of you, my girl. You're doing amazing things. You're making your name as an incredible designer, just like you deserve. And you needed a clean start, after everything that happened with—"

"Do *not* say his name," I cut her off. I didn't need to be reminded about the one guy I nearly risked everything for, the guy who took every ounce of my trust and threw it down the garbage disposal.

"Fine," she conceded. "But you can't beat yourself up for everything that happened with him. He fooled us all."

"Daddy would've seen right through him," I whispered. Nothing made me more embarrassed than knowing that Daddy would've been able to prevent the heartache I put myself through.

Mama paused. "You're probably right. Daddy could always see a person's heart." She sighed. "But don't let yourself think that every man is like Stef—*him*. There are some good ones, too."

"Daddy was the only good one."

"Not the only one, Thea. There are good men, you just have to look."

"Not around here, there aren't." All the guys in Orange County were just like *him*. Snobbish, elitist, materialistic socialites.

Well, maybe that was an exaggeration. Ivy's fiancé, Scott, wasn't so bad. And he was technically part of the elite upper class. But from everything I had seen, he was an outlier. Especially when we were comparing him to men like Ethan Taylor. Ugh. No matter how hard I tried, I couldn't forget how the most handsome man I'd ever seen was also a disgusting pig. Men like him charmed the masses and thought they had everyone fooled. But not me.

I pulled into the dance studio, eager to be done with this conversation. I loved my mom. She had my best interests at heart, that was for sure. And when my dad died eight years ago, she had to fill both roles for me and my little brother, Miles, who was now fourteen. But sometimes a girl needed to be left alone. I was twenty-five, after all.

"I just want you to be happy. And I don't want you to close yourself off to love if the opportunity presents itself. You need friends, people you can trust. And you need to have fun."

I sighed and shut off the car. People I could trust? That was a tough one. "Thanks, Mama. I love you. I'll think about trying to have more fun."

She laughed out loud. "That's the problem. You shouldn't have to think so hard about having fun."

I huffed. "Maybe that's because I don't need fun."

"Mm-hmm," she mused. "All right, my girl. Go have *fun* teaching dance. Be safe."

"I will. Love you, Mama."

"Love you, too." She clicked off the phone, and I headed into the studio. I greeted Clara, who worked at the front desk and headed into Studio A, met by my eight little firecrackers who were waiting patiently. They skipped into the studio, where I warmed them up and started running through their routine.

The choreography was excellent. No surprises there; Ivy was masterful at coaching dance teams and knew exactly what impressed the judges. I took over after she reduced her workload, but my job was just to tighten the details after she choreographed the routine. And that was my expertise. I had the ballet training to notice the slight bends in their knees or toes that were not pointed to their full potential. These final little details made the difference in tenths of points at competitions.

"Girls, you've improved so much," I called out after they ran through it a third time. "But we really need to work on pointing the very tips of your toes." I held out my foot and showed them the difference between pointing my ankle and pointing the tips of my toes. "When your leg is up to your ear, that bit of your toes is so obvious. The judges will see right away if you're not giving it your all. You *have* to make sure you point that last bit."

They all started holding their legs up to their torsos, and I walked around helping them point their toes that last centimeter. Their flexibility would have awed anyone else, but this was normal for someone like me, who had grown up in the dance world my whole life. "You need to practice this at home with a resistance band to strengthen under your toes. You're so close, it will make all the difference."

They nodded. There was a reason they were the elite competitive team. Even though they were feisty little seven- and eight-year-olds, they took dance seriously, practicing and stretching when they were at home. I knew they would improve immensely over the next few weeks before their first competition.

We ran through their dance a few more times, now emphasizing the character and dancing with their hearts. They loved when we worked on that side of the performance. At the end of rehearsal, we were all sweaty and exhausted. They gave me a big group hug and rushed out to their technique classes.

Alone in the studio, I had thirty minutes before Ivy's next class would come in. Lisa, the studio owner, told me I could have the space to dance alone. I scrolled through my Spotify playlist of my favorite contemporary songs and settled on "Let It Be" by the Beatles. The first piano chords rang through the speaker system, and I allowed my body to move to the music.

Ballet was my first love. The grace and strength it required were unmatched. But there was something freeing about applying that grace, strength, and technique from ballet and adding fluidity. And as much as I loved dancing to classical music, I could finally let my authentic emotions flow when I danced to modern music with lyrics.

I danced around the room, sliding, turning, and leaping. Song after song played, and I let myself feel the rhythm and dance. My mind cleared; nothing else worried me.

Until I faced the door and found a very unwelcome visitor. Handsome as ever, leaning against the doorframe, watching me dance like the creeper he was.

Ethan.

Flipping.

Taylor.

Three

THEA

"Agh!" I screamed. "What is wrong with you?"

"Don't stop on account of me." Ethan said, both hands up. "I come in peace." He wore a business shirt with the top button undone and navy slacks. He must have come straight from work, and curse him for looking so good. I watched as his eyes roved down my body, and I instantly regretted wearing my skin-tight leggings today. Still, he hesitated a moment before walking into the studio. He was probably afraid that I would punch him this time and ruin his pretty face.

I smirked, swallowing down my attraction to him. I busied myself with unplugging my phone from the speaker system. "If you're looking for your housefly cousin, she doesn't work here anymore."

He chuckled. His cousin, Blake, had taught here for a few months before I took over. Ivy loved to call her a housefly because her giant sunglasses made her look like an insect. She was obnoxious, entitled, and terrible at her job.

And did I mention she was Ethan's cousin?

She was literally the worst. But no surprise there, considering her family tree.

"I'm not looking for Blake," he replied. His voice rumbled with deep tones. Why did he have to be so handsome? Honestly, he could be the perfect man, if he wasn't such a dirtbag.

I crossed my arms and settled into one hip, looking him straight in the eyes. "What do you want? Trying to pick up a new girlfriend? There are a few single moms outside."

He looked disgusted. "I'm not a fan of cougars."

I shrugged. "Bummer. Now, excuse me, I have to get to my other job." I stepped around him, but he got in my way and put a hand on my shoulder.

"I'm here to talk with you," he said, quickly pulling his hand back. "I have...a proposition for you."

I raised an eyebrow. "I don't think I want to be propositioned by you."

He smoothed the side of his hair. He muttered to himself, something that sounded like "all the wrong things."

"What was that?" I asked.

"Nothing." He crossed his arms over his chest, accentuating his forearms and built chest. Ugh. He was fit, too. "I'd like to make a deal with you."

I blinked a few times, trying to get my bearings. Ivy burst into the room, looking like she was ready to fight someone.

"What is he doing here?" she exclaimed. "Your devil cousin isn't here. You can go find her in Hades."

Ethan laughed out loud. Why did he have to laugh every

time we hated on Blake? "I have no desire to see Blake. But thank you for letting me know."

Ivy looked at me. "Do you need help with him?"

"Nope." I winked at Ethan. "He knows I could take him."

He put his hands up again. "I swear, I mean no harm."

Ivy nodded. "Fine. But I'm teaching in this room, so you need to leave."

Ethan nodded curtly. "Can we talk outside?" he asked me.

I nodded and grabbed my things, then followed him out the door. It seemed I wouldn't get rid of him anytime soon, so I might as well hear what he had to say. He walked up to my car, which looked even more embarrassing next to his silver Porsche. My poor, beat up black Honda next to his shiny piece of perfection was the visual representation of the disparity between the two of us.

Not that I cared.

He leaned back against my car, crossing his arms against his chest. "Have you been to New York for Fashion Week?" he asked.

I furrowed my brow. "Uh, no. I've never had the opportunity."

He nodded. "I figured as much, given your...status."

I saw red and took a sharp breath in through my nose. If only he knew my potential "status" back in San Diego. Before I could reply that I was grateful to not have his "status," he continued. "I think you would enjoy it. With your interest in fashion."

I was taken aback. I didn't think he remembered much about me other than my red hair. And now the fact that I taught ballet. "How would you know about my interests?"

He cleared his throat, looking around the parking lot. "Amy may have mentioned it before."

How Ethan Taylor and Amy Carter were friends was beyond me. I wasn't very close with her, but she was Ivy's best friend, and Ivy was as real as they come. Amy said there was more to Ethan than met the eye, but I couldn't believe her. He'd already shown me his true colors.

"Okay, this has been fun, but I have to work my other job." I pulled out my keys and unlocked my car.

"I need you to come to New York with me," he finally blurted out.

What in the world? I laughed out loud. "You're joking."

"No."

I blinked a few times, waiting for him to explain. "Are you going to elaborate at all? Because, clearly, my answer is no."

He ran a hand over his stubbled face. "I'm trying very hard to use the right words, so I don't scare you off."

"I don't have all day."

He nodded. Slowly, he spoke. "My grandmother holds a benefit every year in Manhattan. It's an important family event, and I'm expected to bring a date. She made it clear that this year she doesn't want me to bring my usual kind of date."

I smirked. "And what does that mean, exactly?"

He met my grin with one of his own. "Her exact word was 'floozies.'"

I laughed out loud. His grandma sounded awesome. "So you're asking me to come...as your date?"

He nodded. "You're the exact opposite of what she would call a 'floozy.'"

I couldn't tell if that was a compliment. Since he usually brought "floozies" around, did that mean I wasn't attractive to him? Not that I would ever want to be classified as a "floozy." Plus, I didn't want to attract his attention.

Right?

"And in return," he continued, "I would take you to Carmen Valencia's show at Fashion Week. I have a few connections and can get you a VIP experience. You could meet designers, go backstage...It could be a great opportunity."

My jaw dropped. I wished I didn't look so affected, but that was an offer I didn't want to refuse. An opportunity to mingle with the most incredible designers? Learning about the latest fashion trends, networking?

But...Ethan. Flipping. Taylor.

I closed my mouth, firming my resolve. "I can't, Ethan. That's an amazing offer, but—"

"But it's me."

I tilted my head. I didn't expect him to be so self-aware. From everything I had seen, he was one of those men who believed he was God's gift to women everywhere.

"I know who I am," he said. "I know how I appear." He opened his mouth to say more, but decided against it.

"Well, thanks for thinking of me," I said, finally pushing him away so I could get into my car. "I hope you find another non-floozy to go with you to New York."

"The problem," he said, swallowing hard, "is that I already told my grandmother about you. She thinks you're my girlfriend."

I laughed out loud. "You want me to pretend to be your

girlfriend? What, does your inheritance depend on it?" This sounded more and more like the lame setup for a rom-com.

"What? No. That's ridiculous." He raked his hand through his hair. "She cares a lot about me. I just want to make her happy."

Well, shoot. That was actually really sweet.

"I'm sorry," I said softly. "I hope she won't be too disappointed."

Ethan stiffened and turned back into his usual self. "The offer still stands," he replied. "I don't have anyone else in mind. I leave a week from today, and the trip is about a week. If you change your mind, here's my number." He offered me his business card.

I waved my hand at him, pushing the card away. "I hope you have a lovely time."

He put the card back in his pocket and stepped away. I closed the door to my car, pulling out of the parking lot and feeling his eyes on me the entire time.

What was with him? Why on earth did he think I would *ever* accept such a crazy offer? Actually, I knew why. Meeting designers was a tempting carrot. But I was no horse. There was no way you could dangle an opportunity like that in front of me in exchange for spending *one week* with Ethan Taylor and pretending to like him. No thank you. I'd happily stay here in Orange County, minding my business.

Right?

I WALKED around the crowd of people, holding a tray full of bruschetta, trying my best to stay invisible. Tonight was an anniversary party, and the guests were still arriving. Why people had anniversary parties on Tuesday nights was beyond me, but I wasn't in charge of scheduling. Besides, this meant I could have another event on the weekend so I could make more money. To buy more fabric. And then pay rent. I had my priorities in order.

Lucas and Amy Carter walked into the room, smiling and laughing. I sighed. My dream was to one day have a love like theirs. They were so comfortable with each other. Lucas was a sweetheart, the classic California surfer boy with sandy blond hair, tan skin, and blue eyes. He looked as good in a suit as he did in board shorts and a tank top. A year ago, he caught the attention of Stella Knight, the world's biggest country star. Now he worked on the music for her latest album. It topped all the charts, but you'd never know it if you talked to Lucas. He was as humble as they came.

His wife, Amy, had deep brown eyes and long brown hair that she curled in soft waves, her gorgeous figure showcased in a gray cocktail dress. She had a great sense of style, growing up as an Orange County socialite, and she was invited to some of the big events around the area. A little over a year ago, she mostly turned her back on everything and everyone when she chose to be with Lucas. Since she was Ivy's best friend, I had hung out with her a few times before, but I wouldn't classify her as one of my personal friends. She ran her own calligraphy business and created a few online courses that were doing well.

Seeing Amy reminded me of her friendship with Ethan. That was one pairing I would never understand. Her brother, Scott, who was engaged to Ivy, mentioned that he and Ethan had some work rivalry, but that he had nothing against Ethan.

I wandered over to Amy and Lucas with the tray, hoping to catch them for a quick conversation. But before I could reach them, Amy pointed at the door and smiled. I looked back, curious who was drawing her attention.

Ethan.

Flipping.

Taylor.

Would this man stay out of my life? My goodness. This was getting out of control. I tried to back away slowly so he wouldn't see me, but he caught my eye and winked at me.

Winked.

He was insufferable.

Regardless, I didn't have to stay and talk to him. But then Amy caught me. "Thea! So good to see you."

I sighed and turned around with a big, fake smile. "Hi, Amy. Good to see you, too." I brought the tray over to her, and she grabbed an appetizer.

"Hello, again," Ethan's voice sounded from behind me. I braced myself for another conversation with him. I could do this. I could be cordial and not throw a big fit. I was mature.

"Hi, stalker," I replied.

Maybe not so mature.

He smirked. "Reconsidering my offer?"

"Never."

"Never say never," he replied.

"Okay, Justin Bieber." I rolled my eyes.

Amy watched our interaction with wide eyes and a small smile on her face. "What am I missing?" she asked. "This looks fun."

I shook my head at her, but Ethan went ahead with the explanation. "I invited her to come to New York with me next week for my grandmother's party."

Amy blinked a few times and exchanged a glance with Lucas. My feelings toward Ethan were no secret, as much as she tried to convince me otherwise. "You invited Thea…" She cleared her throat, deciding to go a different direction. "Gran still does the Save the Pandas benefit? She's a hoot." She turned to me with a twinkle in her eye. "Are you going, Thea?"

"Absolutely not." I took a step back. "I should get back to the other guests."

Amy waved at me, then turned to Ethan and whispered to him. It seemed like she was scolding him, but I couldn't be sure. I had to work, not socialize.

I wandered through the people who entered, offering appetizers and staying invisible. There were always funny tidbits to overhear, like Ethan's mother, Rhonda, telling Maritza Sanchez that Ethan had done pageants as a child. I had to stifle a laugh at the image of a tiny Ethan dressed in a suit, strutting down a runway. Actually, adult Ethan would probably rock it on a runway today.

How unfair.

There was one other server with me tonight. Ashton was about twenty years old, with her brown hair high in a ponytail on top of her head. She was decent at her job, hired to fill Ivy's spot when she quit. I headed into the kitchen to switch out my tray and met Ashton picking up a new tray as well.

"Ugh, one guy here is a total jerk," she said.

"Ethan?" I asked. No one else could be that bad.

"No, Ethan's fine. I haven't seen this guy before." She

pushed the swinging door slightly open and pointed at someone I unfortunately recognized. Dark brown hair, almost black. Baby blue eyes. Tanned skin. A perfectly fitted suit. And *her* on his arm.

But why was he here? He had never attended the events up here in Orange County before. My past was coming to haunt me. I was going to be sick.

"Ashton, can you take his side? Please," I begged. "I'll explain later, but I absolutely cannot interact with him."

She huffed a sigh. "Fine. You owe me."

"Yes, yes. A hundred times, yes. Thank you!" We grabbed our trays and headed out the door. I beelined as fast as I could past them. But I wasn't fast enough.

"Thea? What are you doing here?" His deep voice sounded next to me.

Lord have mercy.

Four

THEA

I turned slowly to face him, pasting a big smile on my face. "Stefan, so good to see you."

"You too." He looked me up and down. "Although I've seen you dressed in much more flattering outfits before." He gave me a wink.

How dare he? He did _not_ have the right to comment on what I wore, let alone reminisce about old times.

Tabitha pulled on his arm. At least she recognized that was out of line. Not that she had any concept of boundaries, either. But I wasn't thinking about that anymore. With long, black hair and blue eyes, they were a perfect pair. Although they looked a little like siblings. But that was their choice, and their problem. Not mine.

Stefan cleared his throat. "Tabby Cat, you've met Thea before, right?" he asked. Blech, what a nickname.

"Yes, of course." She held out her perfectly manicured

hand daintily for me to shake. Her nails looked more like claws. Maybe that's where the nickname came from. "Oh, I'm so sorry. You probably shouldn't fraternize with the guests while you're working. That *is* what you're doing, right?"

I bit my lip. Normally, I wasn't ashamed of the work I did. I was proud of myself, working hard to achieve my dreams. But Stefan had a way of making me feel *lesser-than*. Just like someone else here tonight. Besides, I wanted to leave this conversation as quickly as possible.

"Yep! Working. Having a blast. Good to see you." I turned away from them and nearly collided with Ethan.

"Oh, my lord," I hissed at him. "Why do you keep showing up? You're almost as annoying as your cousin. Shoo, fly!"

He ignored me. "Thea, do you know these people? I'd love an introduction."

Furious, I turned back around. "This is Stefan and Tabitha. I know them from San Diego."

Ethan shook their hands. "Hi, I'm Ethan Taylor."

Stefan's eyes widened. Honestly, I was a little surprised they hadn't met before. They were both in the upper class and only lived an hour apart. But maybe Ethan was more *upper*-upper class. I didn't really keep track of all these minute details.

"I've heard so much about you," Stefan said, gaining his composure.

"And I haven't heard of you at all," Ethan replied. I stifled a little laugh. He could be a jerk, but when he directed his attitude at an even *bigger* jerk, I wanted to cheer. "So how do you know Thea?"

Stefan's eyes darted over to mine. "Oh, well, Thea and I... It's a long story."

"I'll help," I cut in. "Stefan and I were engaged. But he cheated on me with Tabitha." I fluttered my lashes at Stefan and smiled. "That was pretty short, don't you think?"

Ethan chuckled next to me. "Glad to see our Thea has moved on."

Our Thea. What did he mean by that?

"Who do you know here?" he continued.

I backed away slowly, hoping they wouldn't notice, as Stefan pointed at someone who had invited him. Ethan snaked his arm around my waist before I could make an exit.

"I have to work," I said through gritted teeth. I hoped it looked like a smile to everyone else.

"Here, let me help." Ethan took the tray from my hands and turned to the group next to us. "Would you like some appetizers?" he asked them.

I laughed behind my hand as the guests looked at him with confused stares and waved him off.

"See?" he said to me. "We've offered it to someone. Now you can stay and talk." He set the tray down on the table next to us.

"I'd rather not," I whispered.

"I know," he whispered back, leaning his head down to mine. "But roll with it."

I wasn't sure what was happening, or why I listened to him, but I felt oddly comforted by his presence. Stefan had a way of shaking my confidence to nothing, but having Ethan at my side gave me a little bolster.

And I didn't want to admit it, but having Ethan this close made my heart race a tiny bit.

"What do you do for a living?" he asked Stefan.

Stefan puffed his chest a bit. "I'm a lawyer."

"Ah, do you know Bethany Stone? She's a good friend of mine."

I raised my eyebrow at him. "Friend, huh?" I muttered. She was hanging all over him at a few of these events.

He bumped my shoulder with his own. "Yes, friend," he said with a smirk.

Stefan watched our interaction with interest. "Uh, no. I don't know Bethany."

"That's a shame. She's a lovely person." Ethan turned to Tabitha. "And you?"

"I'm a model," she said, flipping her hair over her shoulder. "I'll be walking the runway at New York Fashion Week."

"Oh, that's wonderful. Maybe we'll see you there." Ethan slid his arm around my waist again. A shiver ran down my spine.

I looked up at him in alarm. What was he doing? He winked at me, silently begging me to go along with this.

Might as well see where this goes. I looked back at Stefan and smiled widely, confirming his story. Stefan's eyes widened as he took in our pose and Ethan's words.

"You...you're together?" Stefan stammered. He swallowed, gathering himself. "I mean, you're going to New York together?"

"That's right," Ethan confirmed, smiling down at me. "We'll be in Manhattan for a couple weeks, and I promised Thea I'd take her to Carmen's show at the end. Carmen promised us the VIP experience."

"Carmen...Carmen Valencia?" Tabitha asked, glancing back and forth between us.

I looked up at Ethan. Did he really know Carmen Valencia? She was the hottest up-and-coming designer, but notoriously private. With his connections, I wouldn't put it past him, but did he really call her and set this all up?

"Yes, do you know her as well?" he asked, feigning ignorance.

"I've heard of her, of course," Tabitha said slowly. "But, no, I don't know her personally."

"Ah. She's really lovely. I'd introduce you, but she has very limited availability." He tilted his head at them. "She has time for close friends and family, but considering your history with Thea..." He let his voice trail off.

The tension was so thick, you could cut it with a lightsaber. Stefan and Tabitha's cheeks reddened, and I bit the inside of my cheek to keep myself from laughing out loud.

"Well!" Ethan said abruptly, pulling his hand back and clapping loudly. "It was lovely meeting you. Perhaps we'll see you in a few weeks." He ran his hand down my arm. "I'll talk to you after the event," he said low enough for only me to hear.

I nodded, a little dumbstruck at how he had set Stefan and Tabitha in their place. We definitely needed to talk after this. I waved awkwardly at my least favorite people on the planet and picked up my tray of appetizers so I could go back to my job.

~

A FEW HOURS LATER, I walked out of the banquet hall, exhausted and sore. All I wanted to do was drive home and climb into bed. But once again, Ethan held me back from doing what I wanted. He was leaning on my car, his arms crossed on his chest, waiting to have a conversation. My energy level spiked, anticipating another frustrating conversation with the handsome man who was destined to ruin my life.

"How many times do I have to interact with you today?" I asked.

A half-grin appeared on his face. Curse him for being so handsome.

I scowled. "And what was that with Stefan?"

His grin dropped, and his eyes softened. "I could tell you needed a little help there."

I scoffed. "I don't need help."

"Could've fooled me," he replied. He pushed himself off the car and stood facing me. "You're tough, Thea. I have no doubts about that. But you have to admit, the look on his face when he thought we were together made it worth it."

I couldn't keep my lips from turning up into a smile. "It was pretty awesome," I admitted.

"Going from him to this," he gestured at himself, "is quite an upgrade." He winked at me.

Did he never stop? I rolled my eyes, pushing past him to get to my car.

"Thea, wait," he said, putting a hand on my elbow.

I hesitated. Did I want to wait? Did I want him to explain?

"I wasted three years of my life with Stefan," I whispered, still facing my car. "I've been around this world. I've been around people like you." I turned to face him. "I know who you are. What you want. What you think."

"Let's hear it," Ethan said.

I raised my eyebrows.

"I'm serious," he said. "I asked Amy the same thing a few months ago. Now we're friends. You won't hurt my feelings."

"Fine." I took in a deep breath. "You're arrogant. Self-centered. Materialistic. You think you're better than everyone else, and you get whatever you want." I paused, my eyes dropping to the ground. "Just like Stefan," I murmured.

He was silent for a moment. "You're right," he said. My eyes popped back up to meet his. "At least, the first part. Arrogant. Self-centered. Materialistic." He leaned his head closer to mine and whispered. "But I'm not like him."

Unbidden tears sprang into my eyes. I would *not* cry. Not in front of Ethan Taylor. He didn't deserve it.

Taking in a shaky breath, I backed away from him. "Maybe that's what you think. But the answer is no."

He blinked a few times. "No?"

"No to New York. I'm not coming."

He nodded slowly, giving me space. I took advantage of the opportunity and opened the door to my car, sliding into the driver's seat. I went to close the door, but Ethan's hand held it back.

"If you change your mind, the offer is still open. I leave next Tuesday." He hesitated. "I would really love it if you came."

I still didn't understand why he cared so much, but I'd reached my emotional limit for the evening. "Good night, Ethan."

"Good night, Thea." He closed my door but didn't walk away. As I drove my car out of the parking lot, he watched the entire time, a replay of this afternoon.

I just wanted to get home as quickly as possible and flop into bed, forgetting about this day and all the swirling emotions.

Five

THEA

I checked the clock again. 1:17 a.m. As exhausted as my body was from teaching dance, then serving for hours, my mind would not shut off. I tried everything: listening to calming spa-style music, counting sewing machines in my mind, imagining outfit combinations with the fabric I had on hand. I listened to an audiobook. Nothing worked. I couldn't get Ethan's smirk and Stefan's shocked face out of my mind.

Finally, I embraced being awake and opened Instagram on my phone.

Bad idea.

The first picture that popped up was Amy and Lucas at tonight's event. Which, of course, led my mind back to Ethan and his offer to travel to New York. Why did he care so much? Why did he want me to come? After the night I slapped him, when I made my feelings toward him *very* clear, he kept his distance. I felt his eyes on me every time we were in the same room, but that didn't mean I was the right person to spend an entire week with him in New York.

At the same time, it was New York. New York! Was I an idiot for turning him down? I had spent a couple summers there as a teenager, attending the summer intensive at the Humphrey Ballet School. I knew the city well, and it had a special place in my heart. My love for fashion started there. Walking down Fifth Avenue, admiring the displays in the stores, even trying on clothes at H&M (this was before they even existed on the West Coast) had brought out this hidden desire to create and design.

But still.

Ethan.

Flipping.

Taylor.

The playboy to end all playboys. His mother, the infamous Rhonda Taylor of "True Trophy Wives" fame, was one of the most superficial, obnoxious, materialistic women I had ever encountered. I wished I could say that it was all drama made up for TV, but I had been around her in person. Trust me, that was her true personality. With a mother like that, could I expect any different from Ethan?

Amy's picture on the phone screen reminded me that she had a mother similar to Rhonda. Maybe not quite as terrible, but Ruby King was awful in her own right. Despite her, Amy was a sweetheart. And her brother, Scott, was one of the kindest men I had ever known. He even donated an enormous sum of money to our dance studio to help Ivy's family through a hard time.

But Ethan had shown his true colors, right? The memory

of that night when he tried to seduce me into getting a "ride" in his car made my skin crawl. Disgusting.

I sighed and locked my phone. Instagram was the opposite of helpful. At this rate, there wasn't any point in trying to sleep. I got out of bed and headed to my kitchen. It looked like I'd be sewing instead of sleeping tonight.

Buzz, buzz, buzz.

My eyes fluttered open. *Where am I?* I sat up groggily and looked around at my kitchen, catching the time of 7:15 a.m. on my microwave.

Oh, yes. I had sewn until my eyes couldn't stay open. I didn't know if I wanted to sleep on the couch or in my bed, and I fell asleep at the kitchen table before I could decide.

The buzzing was coming from my phone. I flipped it over and read Ivy's name on the screen. What in the world? This girl was never awake before nine if she could help it. That woke me up faster than cold water on my head, and I answered the call.

"Ivy? Are you okay?" I exclaimed.

"No!" she shouted back.

"Oh, my goodness. What's wrong?"

"Why aren't you going to New York with Ethan?"

I blinked a few times, stunned. Rubbing my eyes, I tried to understand what was going on. "Where did you hear about this?"

"Amy thought it was important enough to wake me up this morning. Ethan told her about it last night."

I rubbed my neck, sore from sleeping awkwardly at my

kitchen table. Such a bad idea, just like going to New York with Ethan. "I'm not going with him because he's a terrible human being."

"Do you really think that?"

"Yes," I replied automatically.

She sighed. "You've never told me why you hate him so much. What if it was just some big misunderstanding?"

"One time, he asked me if I wanted a 'ride' in his Porsche."

Ivy giggled. "What did you say?"

"I slapped him in the face."

She laughed out loud. "Oh, man! Good for you. I wish I had been there." Her laughter died down. "But I have to admit, Amy says he's not nearly as bad as he seems. I think it's an act."

"I've been around these guys before. I know their type."

Ivy hesitated, which was something she rarely did.

"What is it?" I prodded.

"Amy also mentioned some guy and his girlfriend. She saw some interaction with you and them, and Ethan kind of saved the day."

Did these girls tell each other everything? I couldn't keep anything to myself. It was too early for this conversation. "Ex-fiancé. And his new girlfriend."

"You were engaged?!" she shrieked.

"My lord, Ivy! It's too early for your crazy noises."

"Mm-hmm," she hummed. "And this ex-fiancé is... similar to Ethan?"

"Similar enough."

"I see." I could imagine her jiggling her leg. Ivy couldn't stop moving. Short and petite, she had the body and personality of the stereotypical dance instructor. Her blond hair was almost always piled up in a high bun on top of her head, her blue eyes glowing as she enthusiastically encouraged her students.

"Amy is an excellent judge of character," she said. "I mean, look at me. We're best friends."

I couldn't help laughing at that. Sometimes I wished I had Ivy's confidence.

"So if Amy trusts Ethan, I have to believe her," she concluded.

"Why do you care so much?" The moment the words left my mouth, I felt guilty. "I'm sorry, that came out a little harsher than I meant."

"No, I get it. It's not really any of my business, I know. But you always work so hard. Do you ever have fun?"

"You sound like my mom," I muttered.

"Your *mom* is telling you to have more fun? Oh, Thea. That's pretty bad."

"But I enjoy my work!" I protested.

"I know. Trust me, I understand. I love teaching dance, too. But there's still a difference between doing something for fun and doing something to get paid."

I looked around my apartment. Tiny, cramped, messy. Maybe she was right. Maybe a break wouldn't be so bad. It could be a work trip. I'd get inspiration for more sewing projects, make connections with designers, maybe even get some fabric to take home with me.

"Look, Thea," she continued. "I won't tell you what to do. But you saw what happened to me when I overworked myself. We need to take breaks and enjoy life. If we don't, we miss out on the beauty around us." She huffed a laugh. "And we faint at really inconvenient times."

I stifled a laugh. Poor Ivy had worked herself to the bone, trying to provide for her family after a horrible car accident, and fainted while working a catering event with me, only to be filmed and aired on the True Trophy Wives of Orange County television show. It was a turning point for her, leading to accepting the help of others around her and finding love with Scott.

When I thought about it, it wasn't really funny. But Ivy had a great sense of humor and never let life get her down.

Was I heading down the same path? Was I due for a break, just like Ivy?

"I'll think about it," I conceded.

"Yay!" Ivy exclaimed. "Oh, you're going to have the best time."

"I said I'd *think* about it."

"No, no, you're going. And Ethan is filthy rich. You're going to have the best experience."

I scoffed. "I don't want him spending money on me."

"Oh, yes, you do!" she said. "If you hate him as much as you do, then you shouldn't mind spending his money. Besides, you're supposed to pretend to be his girlfriend."

"You're ridiculous," I said, shaking my head. Maybe she was right, though. Why not take advantage of the opportunity?

"Call him and tell him you're coming. I'm so excited for you. And a little jealous. But you deserve it."

"I don't even have his number."

"Hang on." Ivy was silent for a moment. "There. I just texted it to you. Amy prepared me for this."

These girls were impossible. "Fine. I'll call him."

Ivy squealed. "Text me after. I'll come over and help you pack. This is going to be amazing!"

We hung up, and I looked down at my phone in my hands. There was Ethan's number, just like Ivy promised. The decision was up to me.

Ethan confused me with every turn. He was still arrogant and self-assured. But he was using it to help me. Was that such a bad deal?

Pretending to date him, though, would be another story. It would almost be easier if I didn't feel a magnetic pull to him every time he was nearby. But there was something about him that drew my attention, no matter how much I didn't want to admit it.

Having his hands on my waist, holding his hand...Oh, my goodness, would we have to kiss? I'd have to draw the line there.

Even still, maybe it could work. And the benefits I'd get for my career could be life changing.

Was I really going to do this?

I was.

Six

ETHAN

"Ethan!" my father's voice boomed down the hallway. I had barely gotten to work at seven-thirty, which was too late for my father. It was seven or nothing.

I bolted out of my seat at my desk and headed to my father's office. "Hey, Dad. What's up?"

"I have a new assignment for you," he said. "A paper company just declared bankruptcy and needs an assessment of value. I need you to go down there and do the analysis."

"Sounds great," I replied enthusiastically. This could be a turning point in my career. Compared to the menial tasks he usually assigned, an assessment of company value could be my chance to prove my worth.

My phone buzzed in my pocket.

"The manager seems like a complete idiot," he continued, "but you'll figure it out."

I checked my smart watch to see who was calling. It was a San Diego phone number.

San Diego.

Thea was from San Diego.

"Sounds good, Dad." I pulled my phone out of my pocket. "I've got to take this. It's a client."

My dad waved me out of his office. My heart pounded in my chest, praying it was her.

I answered the call. "Hello?"

There was a moment of silence. "Hello, have you considered adding solar to your home?" a man asked.

Disgusted, I hung up the phone and stormed back to my desk. Flipping telemarketers.

I didn't know why I kept waiting for her to call. She was very clear last night that she didn't want to go to New York.

I hoped Amy would get through to her, though. After our conversation last night, she promised she would try to work her magic.

Amy and I watched Thea walk away from us. "Have you told her yet?" she whispered to me.

"Told her what?" I replied.

She rolled her eyes. "Don't pull that on me."

"Told her what?" I repeated.

"That you're crazy about her."

I scoffed and took a sip of my drink.

"Oh, come on. You told me there was some mystery girl when we went on our disaster of a date. Anyone can see how you look at her. I'm surprised she hasn't caught on yet."

I risked a glance over at Thea. She was perfect. Beautiful, poised, intelligent, strong. She was everything I could ever ask for.

Except she hated me.

A year ago, I went about it all wrong. Besides, at the time, I never would have pursued anything lasting with her. But then Amy proved that true love was worth more than social status, and it got me thinking that maybe there was more to life than flashy cars and expensive suits.

Maybe I needed someone to share my life with.

And maybe I could use Amy's help.

"Fine," I consented, looking back at her. "Yes, I like her. Gran told me to bring her with me."

"Gran knows about her?" Amy asked.

"Yes. I can't keep anything from her."

A wide smile appeared on Amy's face. "I'll talk to Ivy. She'll work her magic on Thea."

Amy seemed so confident. I wasn't so sure. But there was a moment, when I had my arm around Thea, defending her from Stefan and Tabby-Cat (most idiotic nickname ever), that I felt her lean into me. I swore there was something there.

I sank into my seat and pulled up my email. My dad had sent the information about the paper company, and I started preparing the questions I would need to ask whoever worked in human resources.

My watch buzzed. A text. I glanced at it quickly.

Hey Ethan. It's Thea. Can we talk?

A thrill of electricity ran down my spine. Maybe she was going to agree. I bolted out of my seat and raced down the aisle, sprinting to the elevator. I didn't want my dad accidentally overhearing this conversation.

As soon as I was outside, I dialed her number.

"Ethan?" Her voice rang in my ear. I couldn't help the grin that spread across my face.

"Hello, Thea," I said as casually as I could manage. "What's up?"

"I decided I'm going to come with you. To New York."

If I wasn't Ethan Taylor, I'd probably pump my fist in the air. But that didn't fit my personality. Instead, I said, "Couldn't resist me after all?"

The second the words left my mouth, I instantly regretted them. When would I learn how to talk to her? She wasn't anything like the prissy Orange County girls I tried to impress. Every word I said pushed her farther away.

"Don't make me change my mind," she replied.

"I wouldn't dream of it."

"But I have one condition," she continued.

I knew where this was headed. "Let's hear it," I said.

"No flirting."

I chuckled. "Yeah, that's not gonna happen."

"Ethan! I'm serious. You're so obnoxious."

Warmth filled my chest. It probably said something about me that my favorite two women, Amy and Thea, were the only ones to call me out. I loved that they saw through my arrogant exterior, where other women would eat it up.

But if this was the only way she'd come to New York, I'd somehow have to tone it down.

"All right. I promise that I'll do my best not to flirt with you—when we're alone. But you understand my grandmother thinks we're dating."

She sighed. "I didn't think about that." There was a pause, and I wondered if she was reconsidering. "Fine. In front of your grandmother, I'll play the role. No kissing, though. In private, keep your grabby hands to yourself. I don't know that I can get any better out of you. And don't get all smarmy and gross. None of those nasty, suggestive comments."

I laughed out loud. "Now that I can agree to." Honestly, I had changed a lot of my flirting methods after her lesson a year ago.

"We leave next Tuesday?" she asked.

"Yeah, that's the plan. Gran has her benefit on Saturday, but she likes to hang out for a few days before. Then Carmen's show is on Sunday, and we'll stay a few days extra with Gran and come home Wednesday."

"Okay." A slight pause. "I'll need a schedule to know what types of events we'll be attending. So I can plan my wardrobe."

"Sure. But..." How could I say this without sounding like a total jerk? "I can provide your wardrobe. So you wouldn't worry about...fitting in."

She laughed. "Ethan. I'm a designer. I don't need your help."

I bit the inside of my cheek to keep myself from saying anything. I'd never seen her outside of her catering uniform and the clothes she danced in at the studio.

Not that I was complaining about the dance clothes.

I knew she was interested in fashion and sewed some costumes, but that didn't necessarily mean she could fit in. Worst-case scenario, I could have a couple of dresses sent to the hotel. We'd make it work.

"All right. Let's have dinner at Magistra's and we can go over the itinerary together," I said.

"No way."

"Why not? I'll treat you to a delicious dinner. You won't have to pay."

"That sounds an awful lot like a date."

Yes, Thea. Yes, it does. "No, no. Just a preview of the things we'll be doing in New York. Only if you want the itinerary."

She grunted on the other end. "Fine. But like I said, no flirting."

"Like I said, I'll try." An idea popped into my head. "I have a condition as well."

"Oh, yeah?" she said. "What is it? Don't embarrass you?"

"Don't fall for me."

Silence.

Laughter erupted in my ear. "Oh, you had me going there." Her giggles wouldn't stop. "You're ridiculous. Don't worry, that won't be a problem."

"Excellent." That was the conversation in every rom-com, right? Some kind of *"don't fall in love with me"* promise, and then they couldn't resist? I figured it was worth a shot. Gran would be proud.

I didn't want to hang up. I wanted to make her laugh all day. But my phone's call-waiting started beeping. My dad was on the other line, probably trying to see where I was. Back to reality.

"I've got to go. But I'll send you that itinerary today. And now you have my number, so you can call any time of day...or night."

"Ew, Ethan. I said no flirting."

The side of my mouth turned up in a grin. "Bye, Thea."

"Bye."

I hung up, not bothering to pick up the call from my dad. I could deal with him inside. Nothing could get me down today, not my dad, and not a moronic paper company manager.

Thea was coming with me to New York.

I PUSHED the itinerary across the table to Thea, in between my old-fashioned and her Mai Tai. "Here are some events we'll be attending."

She glanced down at the document I prepared for her. "Breakfast with your grandmother every morning, meals with your parents...What are these pictures on the side?"

"Ah. Suggested attire for each event."

"You've got to be kidding me," she muttered under her breath. "I'm not an idiot, Ethan."

"I never said you were. I just want to make sure you're dressed appropriately."

"Whatever." She rolled her eyes and set the itinerary aside. "I'll look through that later."

I fought the urge to reopen it and go over each event with her, to ease my mind and know that she understood the requirements of each event. The problem was, you never knew when someone would photograph us. And people in my circle could be highly judgmental about clothing choices. Sure, some people made outlandish choices for the sake of attention, but I did my best to gain attention for being cleanly dressed and well-liked. So far, so good.

Except when it came to Thea.

She sat as far back in her chair as she could, trying to keep away from me. The only other woman to truly treat me like this was Amy, but eventually she came around. I only hoped Thea would see through it all, too.

Thea pulled out her phone and started texting. Ouch. I didn't think dinner was going *that* badly.

"Is there anything in particular you'd like to do in New York?" I asked, trying to draw her attention back to me.

She shrugged.

"There are some open blocks of time," I said, gesturing at the itinerary. "How about—"

Her phone started ringing, and she held up a finger, cutting my question off.

"Hey, Ivy." She paused. "What? No way! Oh, that's terrible. No, I'll be there right away." Thea hung up the phone and stood up, dodging the waitress who had just arrived to serve our shrimp appetizer. "So sorry. Dance studio emergency. You know how it is."

"I assure you, I do not." An amused smirk emerged on my face. I could see through this all. She hadn't even touched her drink, knowing that she was going to escape soon and needed to drive. I had to admire her dedication to stay away from me as much as possible.

"Just crazy timing, you know?" she continued, folding the itinerary and tossing it into her purse.

"Yes, crazy. You'd almost think it happened on purpose."

"Oh, no, of course not. You know I'd never try to skip out on a dinner with *you*." Her eyes narrowed at her last word, daring me to contradict her.

I knew she was trying to be aggressive, but her fire just made me want her more. "Of course. You'd never try to get away from an evening with me."

"Exactly." She nodded in agreement. "Well, I'll see you

next Tuesday." She stepped toward the exit, then turned back and grabbed a shrimp, popping it in her mouth with a wink. I raised my glass to her, and she turned to the exit.

I took a sip of my old-fashioned and watched her leave with a smile on my face. New York was going to be a challenge, but I couldn't wait.

Seven

THEA

I breathed a little easier as I exited the restaurant. At least Ethan hadn't insisted on picking me up, otherwise I'd be stuck here without my car. I had to pay for the valet, which was annoying, but it was worth it to leave before things got more awkward.

I called Ivy back as I waited for my car. "Thank you, you're a lifesaver."

"You're ridiculous," she said. "Sometimes I think *I'm* ridiculous, and then you do something crazy like that."

"You don't even understand. He printed out an itinerary that had an image of 'appropriate attire' next to each event."

Ivy cackled. "He *is* well-dressed. Even you have to admire him for that, Miss Designer."

Of course I did. But I wasn't about to admit that to Ivy. "It's the implication that I don't know how to be well-dressed."

"Fair enough. Do you know where you're staying yet?"

I glanced down at the itinerary and widened my eyes as I read the name of the hotel. "Park Fifth Hotel," I said. It was right across from Central Park, and one of the most luxurious hotels in Manhattan. I had been inside the lobby once or twice, but could never afford to stay there. One point in the right direction.

"That's awesome," Ivy said. "I've seen it on the Trophy Wives Show."

"Yeah, that's at least one positive."

"And don't forget what you're getting out of this. You're going to meet Carmen Valencia. Come on, girl! It's Fashion Week!"

"You're right," I admitted. Fashion Week. New York. I could even take a ballet class or two at the Humphrey Ballet School. I had checked their website and saw a few open adult ballet classes on the schedule. According to Ethan's itinerary, I had some open windows that would allow a class or two. My favorite teacher from ten years ago, Nicole Jameson, was teaching open adult classes now. She bucked tradition as the second African American professional ballerina ever, and her insights were invaluable. Even when I knew my curves took me out of the running as a professional ballerina myself, she took me aside and promised me there was a place for me in the dance world, too. Maybe I'd have to find my own role, but my time as a dancer wasn't over. And she was right.

I said goodbye to Ivy and drove the rest of the way home. I unlocked my door and glanced around my living room. There wasn't much to see except yards upon yards of fabric. I'd probably be able to afford a nicer apartment if I didn't blow my paychecks on sewing materials, but at times like these, my obsession with beautiful patterns and textures came in handy.

Because I had a wardrobe to create.

Tuesday came before I knew it. I stood outside my apartment, suitcases nearby, waiting for Ethan to come pick me up. At 8:55 on the dot (his scheduled time of arrival), a huge silver Escalade pulled into my apartment parking lot. The driver, an older man with a kind smile, opened the back door for me. I pulled my bags toward the trunk, but he gently waved me off and told me to get in the car.

I expected to see Ethan's parents, but only Ethan greeted me.

"This huge thing is just for us?" I asked.

He gave his signature half-smirk and shrugged. "This way, you don't have to worry about me getting too close." He winked, and I rolled my eyes, settling into the seat across from him.

"My father is working today, and my mother had an appointment, so my parents are coming Thursday night," he explained. "But Gran likes to spend extra time with me."

"Workaholic Nicholas Taylor didn't want to take extra time off? Shocking," I replied.

Ethan huffed a laugh, but his expression soon turned serious as he looked at me closely.

"What?" I asked, suddenly self-conscious. I tugged at my crop top, trying to hide the tiny sliver of skin that showed above my maxi skirt. It was a tame outfit, a white crop top with a flowy teal chiffon maxi skirt, but Ethan's gaze made me feel like I was wearing a bikini.

His eyes met mine with a twinkle. "I'm not supposed to be flirting. So maybe I shouldn't say anything." And then he winked.

My face erupted in flames. Knowing that he was holding himself back from flirting made him even more attractive.

No, Thea. You are not attracted to Ethan Taylor. Well, okay. You're attracted to him. But nothing's going to happen. He's just another Stefan.

The driver got back into his seat, taking me from my thoughts. I pulled my long, red hair over my shoulder and neutralized my face. "Thanks for not flirting."

He held my gaze a moment longer and gave a quick nod as the car jolted forward.

The drive to the airport was mostly silent. Ethan was doing something on his phone, but I couldn't look at mine or read anything without getting carsick, so I popped in one earbud and blasted Taking Back Sunday. I could use some of their angst right now to fight against my attraction to Ethan.

I wished I could sketch in a moving car, but ever since I was little, I got the worst motion sickness. My mom told stories about me throwing up all over my car seat as a toddler, and I couldn't think too long about that before wanting to throw up myself. So music it was.

We arrived at the airport thirty minutes later, and Ethan and I were dropped off at the curb. He headed straight to the first class check-in line, and a big grin spread across my face. I hadn't processed that we'd be flying first class, but now I couldn't wait.

Glancing around the airport, I realized we were being

watched by ten to fifteen people. One woman even had her phone out.

"Are they taking pictures of you?" I whispered.

He nodded. "When your mom is a Trophy Wife, and you've been on the show a few times, you get noticed. Especially here at home. In New York, it shouldn't be so bad." He waved at a couple of the women and gave them a wink, at which they squealed.

Ugh. Just another reminder of why I despised men like him. I rolled my eyes and turned my back to them, hoping they hadn't tried to get a picture of me, too.

Ethan eyed me curiously. A wicked grin lit his face, and he turned me by the shoulders to face the women. "This is Thea!" he called out. "Isn't she gorgeous?"

I was going to kill him.

I turned my head to him to tell him off, but he whispered in my ear, making chills run down my spine. "Stefan and Tabitha might see this. It's best if we sell it."

He made a good point. I didn't want to run into them at Fashion Week, only for them to say that they saw a picture of me pushing Ethan off. I flashed Ethan a big smile, then looked back at the women and shrugged.

And then, before I could stop him, he slid his hands around my waist, pressed his chest against my back, and gave me a kiss on the cheek. I'd be lying if I said I didn't lean into him, reveling for a moment in the warmth of his touch.

The women looked disappointed that he had someone with him. Did they think he'd really be interested in them? It was Ethan Taylor. He had a date everywhere he went. Besides, these women had to be his mother's age. It was a little scary that they were so obsessed with him.

"Excuse me?" the woman at the desk called. We had been too distracted to notice that it was our turn. I heaved my giant bags up on the scale.

"You brought a lot with you," Ethan commented.

"I'm a designer. Of course I brought wardrobe options."

He smirked. "Hopefully you won't stand out too much at the events."

I put my hands on my hips and turned to face him. "Ethan Taylor, you need to stop that. If you didn't have confidence in my ability to put together an outfit, you shouldn't have brought me with you. You're insulting my fashion sense, which is pretty fundamental to my personality."

He blinked a few times, his cheeks turning red. His mouth opened, shut, then opened again. "I...I'm sorry."

The attendant looked back and forth between us. "I...uh... need some ID."

Ethan and I quickly pulled our driver's licenses out of our bags and silently set them on the counter. The attendant worked quickly and handed us our boarding passes.

We waited awkwardly in the security line, not saying a word to each other. Since we were First Class, we zoomed to the front of the line and got through right away.

"Do you want to hang out in the VIP lounge area?" Ethan finally asked, breaking the silence.

"Sure," I replied, following him into a hidden entrance with a lounge that overlooked the tarmac. Huge, comfy chairs spread across the room, and a coffee machine sat in the corner.

"Do you want a drink?" he asked, pointing to the bar.

I laughed despite my annoyance with him. "It's nine thirty in the morning. I'll just have coffee."

He nodded, and we found a pair of seats near the window. The silence hung thickly between us, but I had no intention of apologizing to him for my sharp tone. He needed to be set in his place, and I wasn't about to minimize his rudeness to make him feel better.

"When I was eight," Ethan suddenly began, sitting forward in his seat, "I was really into Pokémon. Like, obsessed. I wanted to be Ash." He wasn't looking at me, his eyes off in the distance as he remembered. "I would run around my house pretending to catch Pokémon. That's the life of an only child."

My lips turned into a small smile. I had been an only child for a while, too, but I wasn't ready to say that. I was still mad at him. Maybe, if he redeemed himself, I'd tell him how Peter Pan was my imaginary boyfriend and I got married to him every morning when I was four years old.

"My parents held a party at our house. I have no idea what it was for. They constantly had parties, and they expected me to show up and hide in a corner." He shook his head. "I figured no one would notice me, and I wanted to wear my favorite new shirt. It had Ash and Pikachu on the front. I came downstairs, in the middle of all these socialites in their tuxes and gowns, and my dad took one look at me and pulled me by the arm up to my room. He yelled at me about the importance of proper attire, and that I was an embarrassment to the family." He took in a shaky breath. "I had to stay in my room alone for the rest of the night. They didn't feed me or anything. And I wasn't allowed to attend another event until I was thirteen."

He finally looked over at me. "I guess that's why I'm always so concerned about proper attire."

My heart broke for little Ethan. How must he have felt? Hungry, abandoned, and alone? I could only imagine him crying in the corner of his room, waiting to have one special thing that was his.

Tentatively, I placed a gentle hand on his forearm, and his eyes flicked down to where I touched him. "I'm sorry that happened to you," I said softly. "I bet your shirt was amazing."

He looked back up at me and smiled widely. "It was pretty epic. But I never wore it again."

"Not even to school?"

He shook his head. "I had to wear a uniform. Besides, I threw it away after that night. I couldn't look at it anymore."

Poor Ethan.

I felt the need to reassure him, even though I wasn't thrilled by the way he directed his insecurities at me. "I promise my outfits will be appropriate." I paused a moment. "And if it's any consolation, you're always best-dressed at the events I've catered."

"Oh, yeah?" He winked. "Couldn't help noticing me, huh?"

"I had to make sure you kept your grabby hands to yourself."

He chuckled. "Don't worry. I learned my lesson." He settled back in his chair, looking out the window.

Did he really? He didn't seem quite as bad as I remembered, especially on the night I slapped him. I couldn't be sure if there was a genuine change, though.

We sat and people-watched in comfortable silence. Something had changed between us. With that revelation from his past, I saw Ethan Taylor in a new light. He was still arrogant and superficial, but maybe that came from his upbringing. Maybe growing up with parents who cared more about their appearances than their own son shaped him into the man he was today.

And was that who he truly was? Or was that the facade he wore for the world to see?

I couldn't be sure. But I also didn't like that Ethan Taylor was slowly redeeming himself in my eyes.

Eight

ETHAN

We waited together in the VIP lounge for a little while before heading to the gate for our flight. My dad, the picture of punctuality, had always ingrained in me to arrive at least two hours before a flight, even at a slow airport like John Wayne. But sitting with Thea was better than sitting alone, or even worse, with my parents.

After I told her my Pokémon story, she relaxed. I could see her expression change a bit toward me. Maybe it was a little bit of pity, but she also seemed more comfortable. I was going to roll with that as long as possible.

We were the first ones on the flight since we were in First Class. Thea sat back in her window seat and closed her eyes. After I put our carry-on bags into the overhead compartment, I stood watching her for a moment without her knowledge.

"I could get used to this," she murmured.

I smiled down at her, glad that I could give her this experience. The sight of her still took my breath away. I always thought she was beautiful, even in her catering uniform, but seeing her with her hair down and clothes that accentuated her curves brought her to a new level. I tried not to stare at the tiny centimeter of skin she showed between her crop top and skirt on the car ride to the airport, but I wasn't very successful.

I settled into my seat next to her. "First class has its perks."

A buzzing noise came from her bag. She sat up and checked her phone, then cursed quietly under her breath. "It's my mom. I have to take it." I nodded.

"Hey, Mama," she answered. I could hear a frantic voice on the other side of the line, with the words "airport" and "Ethan Taylor" coming through.

"Yeah, Mama. Sorry, I forgot to tell you." She looked over at me with a weak smile, knowing I could hear. Her eyes dropped into her lap as she listened more. "I'm sorry you found out like that." Another pause. "No, it's not really like that. We're..." Her eyes flicked over to me, then back to her lap. "We have a deal."

Her eyes widened as her mom kept talking. "Mom!" she hissed. "I am *not* his escort!"

Before she could protest, I grabbed the phone from her hands. "Hello, Thea's mom. This is Ethan Taylor."

"Hello, Ethan," a sweet but stern voice rang through the phone. "Why is my daughter at an airport with you?"

"I'm taking her to New York with me," I answered. "She's coming to my grandmother's benefit as my platonic date, and I'm taking her to New York Fashion Week in return."

She paused. "And what exactly are you asking of her?"

"Nothing sexual, I promise you that," I said with a grin. A few passengers standing in the aisle looked over at me, and I waved at them. Thea buried her face in her hands. "But we are playing a bit of a charade with my grandmother. She thinks Thea is my girlfriend. Don't worry, though. Thea has made me promise not to flirt with her."

She laughed. "That sounds like Thea." She paused a moment. "But maybe a little flirting wouldn't hurt."

I widened my eyes in surprise. Was she *trying* to get us together? "I'm not sure I understand."

"Thea needs to have a little fun. And after everything that has happened over the last few years, she deserves it. Just...make sure she has fun, okay? But, you know, within boundaries."

What happened over the last few years? It sounded like more than just a broken engagement. I looked over at Thea, keeping my eyes locked with hers as I answered. "I'll do my best."

"And if you do anything to hurt her, I'll make sure you're never capable of having children."

So that's where Thea got it from. "Understood."

"Good. Now I'd like to speak with my daughter."

I handed the phone back to Thea. "Hey, Mama," she said weakly. She listened for a few more seconds, inserting a "Mm-hmm" or "Okay" until finally a "*Mom!*" burst loudly from her lips, drawing the attention of the passengers standing in the aisle.

She cleared her throat. "Okay, that's enough. I'll talk to you later." She hung up the phone and put it on airplane mode, then leaned over and stuffed it into her bag.

"So, your mom is interesting," I said.

She sat up slowly and bit her bottom lip. I forced my gaze on her eyes. "That's one way to describe it," she replied.

"She threatened my manhood."

She nodded, a small smile on her lips. "That sounds right."

"She's pretty protective, huh?"

"Yep." She locked eyes with me, hesitating. Her mouth opened and closed once, then she spoke. "My dad died a few years ago. It's just her, me, and my brother. So, we're pretty tight."

That was a piece of the puzzle I hadn't known before. "I'm sorry about your father," I said, not sure what else to say.

"Thank you. We've done our best to manage without him." She ran a hand through her hair. "Anyway, she wants what's best for me, whether or not I agree with her."

"You didn't tell her you were going to New York?" I asked.

"I told her I was going to New York. I just didn't mention who I was going with."

"And how did she find out?"

"I guess a picture of us is on Instagram. One of her friends sent it to her."

"Ah." I nodded. "And what got you so worked up?"

She blinked a few times, pretending to be distracted by the passengers in the aisle. "Nothing."

"Oh, come on." I nudged her arm, bringing her attention back to me. "I told you about Pokémon. You can tell me this."

She blushed furiously. "She said you were hot and that I should go for it."

I felt my mouth turn up into a huge grin. "That wasn't so difficult, was it?" I said, settling back into my seat.

"Oh, it was. Because I knew this was how you'd react."

I laughed. "And how am I reacting?"

"Like a peacock being told he's pretty."

I winked at her. "I am a pretty peacock. Don't forget it."

She rolled her eyes and faced forward. "Fashion Week, Fashion Week," she muttered.

"What?" I asked.

"Just reminding myself why I'm doing this."

I chuckled. If I had any say, there was more than just Fashion Week on the line.

THE FLIGHT WAS MOSTLY UNEVENTFUL. Thea chose a dance movie, and I chose the latest superhero action flick. No matter how old I got, something about saving the day always appealed to me. Maybe that's why I got such a kick out of defending Thea in front of Stefan.

She fell asleep for the last hour and rested her head against the window. I wished she would feel comfortable enough to rest her head on my shoulder. But I could tell I was making some headway in her comfort level with me. A week ago, she wouldn't have said more than one word to me if she could help it.

I watched her without her knowledge, which I knew sounded creepy. But I couldn't help myself. Her layers were slowly unraveling, and I was getting a peek at who she was inside. I knew nothing about losing a parent, or even a grandparent, but despite the loss she constantly carried around, she was strong and determined. And beyond that, she had been *engaged*. But he cheated on her.

I wondered how she could carry herself with so much dignity, despite having endured so much heartache. All I wanted was to ask her myself, but I had to take my time. It was hard enough for her to share those pieces of her life with me.

The plane landed around eight-thirty at night. The time change was a little jarring at first, but we'd benefit in the end. We would be alert in the evenings, when all the action was happening in the city. Thea and I got off the plane, gathered our bags, and I found a familiar face holding a sign that said "Taylor."

"Hayk! So good to see you," I said, patting our driver on the back. "Is your wife feeding you well?"

"Always," he said with a smile. I'd known him since I was a little boy, and his waistline only grew as his hair continued to gray. Mine would too, if I was fed that amazing Armenian food every day.

"She sent some dolma for you to eat in the car," he added.

My mouth watered at the thought. Even the most expensive restaurants I had been to couldn't match her stuffed grape leaves.

I introduced him to Thea, and they shook hands. He looked her over, then winked at me and gestured to head out of the airport.

"She's not like your other girls," he whispered to me, Thea trailing behind.

"How could you tell?" I asked.

"She's not putting her hands all over you," he replied.

I huffed a laugh, glancing over at Thea, who was looking around the airport with light in her eyes.

"And you watch her."

I snapped my head over to Hayk, who was more perceptive than I had previously given him credit for. "You might be right."

"I know these things," he said. "I picked out my wife when I was thirteen."

I grimaced. "That's a little much."

He shrugged. "I just knew." He looked back at Thea as he continued walking. "Thea, have you been to New York before?"

She nodded. "A few times. I spent four summers in the Humphrey Ballet School's trainee program."

Hayk widened his eyes at me. "A ballerina?" he whispered.

I nudged him with my arm. "That's enough meddling. Let's get to the car."

Laughing, he stepped outside and led us to his black Escalade. The muggy air hit us hard, and Thea fanned herself. We were so used to the dry California heat, but New York felt like someone had wrung out a wet towel over us. Hayk loaded our bags into the trunk, and Thea and I stepped over to the side. I offered her my hand to climb into the giant car, but she waved me off. I smirked. Figures. I should've known better than to offer Thea a hand.

I hopped into the seat next to her and found the Tupperware with the dolma. Opening the lid, I took in a big whiff of the delicious grape leaves, meat, parsley, and onion. Thea tried to not look interested next to me.

"Ever had dolma?" I asked.

"I thought I had," she replied. "But that looks different."

"It's Armenian dolma," I explained. "They stuff the meat

and rice inside the grape leaves, then cook it and serve it warm. It's my favorite food in the world, and no one makes it like Hayk's wife." I wagged my eyebrows at her. "You know you want to try."

She glanced between my face and the food, and I knew she was as hungry as I was. We had a few snacks on the plane, but nothing substantial. "Fine," she relented. She picked one up and made an attempt at a dainty bite, but the tomato juice went all over her face and skirt. "Oh, no!" she exclaimed.

Without thinking, I laughed and swiped my thumb under her bottom lip to clean her mouth. Her eyes widened in surprise, but she didn't push my hand away. I took a gamble and lightly brushed her bottom lip, too.

The driver's door opened, startling both of us. I settled back into my seat, and Thea looked out the window. "To the Park Fifth Hotel?" Hayk asked, looking back at me with a wink.

"Yes, thanks," I muttered. *And thanks for the interruption.*

As the car pulled away from the curb, Thea looked over with daggers in her eyes. Her perfect lips mouthed the words *No flirting.*

So close.

Nine

THEA

The drive into Manhattan took about thirty minutes, but it always felt too long. When I first flew here at fourteen, I thought the airport was in the city. Now I realized how silly that was, since Manhattan was an island, and an overcrowded one at that. Still, every time the plane landed, I wished I could step out of the airport and into the hustle and bustle of the city.

Since it was past nine at night, the lights were my favorite part. Even before we were actually in the city, the buildings lit the way, welcoming us in. I had no idea how Hayk could navigate the giant Escalade through the New York City traffic, but he was calm and confident as he honked and careened around the little yellow taxis, keeping up a steady stream of conversation with Ethan about his grandmother. It turned out Hayk was her regular driver, and he had known Ethan since he was a little boy. There was an interesting level of comfort between the two of them I wouldn't have expected. I expected him to think Hayk was beneath him, not worth a second glance. Instead, he treated him like an uncle he missed dearly over the last year.

Ethan threw me for a loop, that's for sure.

Finally, Hayk pulled up to the Park Fifth Hotel, and Ethan climbed out. I tried to keep a comfortable distance from him during the flight, especially after his conversation with my mother and her insistence that I "don't push away the most gorgeous man who has been in my presence." Her words, not mine.

Why I decided to tell him about my father, I wasn't quite sure. Maybe because he shared a piece of himself with his childhood story, I felt the need to reciprocate. But I wasn't about to pour out my deep, dark thoughts to him. Because my current deepest, darkest thought was how much his touch stirred emotions I hadn't felt...ever.

That thumb across my lip.

Fire. Fire everywhere.

Thank goodness Hayk interrupted us, because I was not thinking clearly. I needed to remind myself, once again, who I was dealing with here. It didn't matter if he was obsessed with Pokémon and superheroes (yes, I saw what he was watching on the plane). Maybe he was a little boy at heart who didn't get the chance to enjoy the things he loved, but need I remind you again who we're talking about?

Ethan.

Flipping.

Taylor.

I got out of the Escalade and saw the giant spot of tomato juice on my skirt. I nearly groaned out loud. It wasn't a difficult make—this skirt probably took me all of fifteen minutes to sew together—but it was the last bit of this fabric I had, and it perfectly matched my top. I'd do my best to get the stain out, but it didn't look promising.

Hayk handed our bags to the bellhop, which was the first time I processed just how ratty my old suitcases were. Pairing that with the stain on my skirt, I clearly didn't belong here. With a hearty handshake for Ethan and a little bow to me, Hayk headed out.

"I'm going to head to the restroom and see if I can handle this situation," I whispered to Ethan, gesturing at my skirt.

He grimaced at the stain. "Good idea," he agreed.

I turned to search for a bathroom, but he grabbed my arm and turned me back around. I couldn't help the little gasp that emerged. "Thank you," he said, his eyes searching deep into mine. "I know you think my concern with attire is silly. Trust me, I'm working on it. But I appreciate your consideration."

"Believe it or not, I actually care about my clothes being stained," I said with a smile. "I'm not as clueless as you think."

He let me go, heading over to the reception desk, and I found the most lavish bathroom ever. Gold fixtures, pristine white counters, and a giant gold frame around the mirror. Taking a deep breath, I looked myself over. My outfit, minus the stain, was still pretty chic. But the rest of me looked like I had been traveling for the last eight hours. Which was accurate.

I gently blotted the stain as best as I could, which just made it look like I had wet myself. Lovely. This hotel was too fancy for air dryers, so I used the terry towels to squeeze out the remaining water. To be honest, I wasn't sure if there was any improvement, but I was out of options. I slung my purse in front of me, trying to conceal the wet spot, and headed out the door.

I was just in time, because Ethan was walking toward me with the keys in hand. "All done?" he asked, glancing down at my skirt.

I pulled my purse away. "Not exactly, but I'll try to fix it in my room."

He nodded, then gestured for me to walk with him to the elevators.

A horrific realization came over me. Did his grandmother make the reservations? In a panic, I squeaked, "We're not in the same room, are we?"

He peered over at me quizzically, then a smile lit his eyes. "No. Gran is too old-fashioned to allow an unmarried couple to stay in the same room."

Phew. Thank goodness for old-fashioned Gran.

I nodded, excited to spend the next few hours in solitude. As much as I enjoyed teaching dance and being around the kids, I really needed time alone to recharge. As soon as I got into my room, I was going to change into some comfy pj's and watch TV. By myself.

We got off the elevator on the nineteenth floor (almost the top!) and I followed Ethan down the hall. Lavish carpet in royal hues covered the floor, and more golden frames decked the walls.

"Here's your room," Ethan said, pulling the card from his pocket.

I put a hand on his arm. "One more rule," I said. He raised

a brow in anticipation. "My room is my personal space. You're not welcome in there."

"We'll see about that," he said with a wink.

"Ethan! Flirting!"

"Sorry, sorry." He opened the door and held it as I stepped in. I had to hold back a gasp. This was the most beautiful room I had ever stayed in. It had a couple of sitting chairs, a coffee table, and a little kitchen table. There was a chandelier above the couches, delicate but ornate.

I sauntered through the room, finding a giant king size bed with the fluffiest white comforter I'd ever seen. I was in heaven. While I was busy taking in my surroundings, the bellman came to the door and dropped off my suitcases, and I caught Ethan giving him a generous tip out of the corner of my eye.

"Well, I guess I should get to my room," Ethan said, putting his wallet back in his pocket. He gestured towards a door in the living room. "We actually have adjoining rooms, so if you need anything, you can knock."

Yeah, that wouldn't happen.

"Thanks," I said. He nodded and followed the bellman out of my room. Finally. I was free of Ethan Taylor.

I fell backwards onto the comforter, arms wide, and it was like floating on a cloud. This really was amazing.

But what now? It may have been almost ten in New York, but my body was still in California time. My stomach grumbled, reminding me I hadn't eaten anything for dinner other than the dolma that exploded all over my skirt.

I sat up, glancing around my room for a solution. A menu on the desk winked at me. Yes! I could order room service.

And considering that I wasn't paying for the room, I could indulge, right?

I was debating between a cheeseburger and a personal pizza when a knock sounded on the adjoining door. I got out of my bed and walked over.

"Yes?" I called through the door.

"You don't want to open up and talk to me?" Ethan replied.

"Not particularly."

"Just afraid you won't be able to resist, right?"

I rolled my eyes, even though he couldn't see. "What do you want?"

He hesitated a moment. "I was checking if you wanted to grab something to eat. I figured you were hungry."

Again, he was confusing me from one moment to the next. Here I was, figuring out how to feed myself on his tab while avoiding him at all costs, and he made sure I was taken care of. But I never knew with Ethan and his ulterior motives.

"I was going to order room service and stay in. I'm wiped."

"Oh. Okay." The silence stretched out, and I assumed he had walked away. I took a step back over to my bed to make my final decision.

"Thea?" Ethan's voice called me back.

"Yes?"

"Good night. Thank you for coming with me."

I sucked in a breath, my heart speeding up the tiniest bit. Why did he make me so unsettled? "Good night, Ethan."

A pit settled in my stomach as I flopped onto my bed. Was I wrong to want to eat alone? I didn't owe Ethan anything, did I? I was doing *him* a favor by coming to New York and being his date. And he was repaying the favor by taking me to Fashion Week. End of story.

With a determined nod, I decided on a burger. I just hoped it wouldn't make the pit in my stomach any worse.

~

AT EIGHT THE NEXT MORNING, a knock on the adjoining door echoed through the room.

"Thea? Are you ready for breakfast?"

"I'm not feeling well," I called back.

Lies. I was sitting on my bed, fully dressed and ready for the day. I just didn't want to face Ethan and his grandmother.

Last night, while I was waiting for my cheeseburger (which wasn't as delicious as I had hoped), I found the picture of me and Ethan at the airport that was circulating on social media. Well, more like Ivy sent it to me with a million heart-eyed emojis, and I had to tell her it was just pretend.

Except when I looked at the picture myself, I couldn't justify it completely. The look in Ethan's eyes was full of pure adoration. Had Stefan looked at me like that? I couldn't think of *anyone* ever giving me those eyes. Ethan's attention was focused and heated, and while he took it overboard sometimes, there was something flattering about it, too.

So it was no wonder I woke up this morning in a cold sweat, dreaming about Ethan's thumb skimming my bottom lip, which turned into incredibly hot kisses. There was no way I could face him right now. I wished there was something I could do to turn off my subconscious attraction to him. So far, nothing.

"Oh, no," he called back. "You're really sick?"

"Yep." Nope.

He paused for a beat. "Do you need anything?"

The genuine concern in his voice made me feel a twinge of guilt. "I'm just going to rest in the room. I'm so sorry I'm going to miss breakfast. Hopefully I'll feel better in the afternoon."

"All right," he said, sounding resigned. "I'll come check on you later."

"Thank you."

A moment later, I heard his door open and shut, and his footsteps sounded down the hallway. I counted to five hundred before emerging from my room and scurrying to the elevator.

Okay, maybe I felt a little guilty. But I didn't know how I felt about Ethan. I just needed a break from him after being overloaded yesterday. A few hours alone would be helpful to reset. Besides, we were right across from Central Park, and all I wanted was to stroll around the park with a cup of coffee.

I headed out of the lobby and grabbed an iced coffee from a stand nearby. The muggy air wrapped around me as I walked across the street to Central Park. I headed toward The Pond, one of my favorite places to hang out when I was here in my summer program. The Pond itself was below street level, so it was really beautiful to watch from above and see the different species of birds that made it their home.

I walked along the path, sipping my coffee and people watching. I didn't pay attention to my direction and was disappointed when I realized I had accidentally looped back around to the beginning of my path. Looking around for my next direction, someone unexpectedly caught my eye.

Ethan.

Flipping.

Taylor.

And his grandmother.

Feeding...pigeons?

Ten

ETHAN

"Thea?" I called. That couldn't be her, right? She said she wasn't feeling well.

But a year of keeping watch on her from afar taught me how to point her out in any crowd. Maybe that was a little creepy, but it was the truth. I had memorized her hair color, the poise that came from being a former ballerina, the curve of her body...

Okay, that was extremely creepy.

But what really sealed the deal was how she ran away as soon as she saw me and Gran.

"Thea!" I called louder, breaking into a run to chase after her. I could hear Gran cackling behind me.

She may have been a dancer, but she was not a very good runner. I caught up to her pretty quickly, gently tugging on her arm. "Thea! Are you feeling better?"

Her eyes darted around nervously. "Uh, yes! Better. Much better. The fresh air helped."

I noticed her holding a cup of iced coffee with some seriously melted cubes. "I wonder how long it took for you to feel better after I left for breakfast."

She laughed tightly. "Oh, you know. Just needed, uh... some air."

"You know, running away from me doesn't look good for this whole 'fake dating' scenario," I reminded her. Even if it wasn't true, she needed to be put in her place.

She gulped, looking over my shoulder at Gran. "Is...is that your grandmother?" She pointed at Gran in alarm.

I looked over my shoulder to see Gran with her hands outstretched, a flock of pigeons encircling her.

"Ah. Yes." I nodded at her. I held out my hand. "Come meet her. And pretend you like me a little."

Reluctantly, Thea put her hand in mine and walked in step toward Gran. Something about her hand in mine felt so right. Yes, I knew it was fake, but the warmth that pulsed from her palm felt like home.

"She likes to feed the pigeons every Tuesday," I explained as we walked.

"That's not...dangerous?"

"Oh, it definitely is. And very frowned upon. But no one would dare tell a little old lady to stop feeding pigeons."

"I heard that," Gran called over to us. "Don't you dare call me old."

"You're the one who said you were dying," I called back.

Thea looked at me in alarm.

"It was a joke. Gran's fine." We reached Gran and her pigeons, and I made the official introduction. "Gran, this is Thea."

"Hello, Thea. I'm Rita," she said, her eyes twinkling. "I've heard so much about you."

"Oh?" Thea asked. "Good things, I hope."

She tittered a laugh. "Yes, of course. But I also hear you keep Ethan on his toes. I like that." She punctuated her statement with a wink. "So, it seems you're feeling better. Ethan said you were bedridden this morning."

"Uh, yes." She swept her hand through her hair. "I really felt terrible. But it turns out I needed some fresh air."

"Perfect! You can join us for the rest of our walk."

"Oh, no, I'm feeling a little winded—"

"Nonsense." Gran tucked Thea's arm in hers, which was a little awkward because she was so short. Thea looked at me for help, but I just shrugged. I wasn't about to help her after the charade she pulled this morning.

Breakfast with Gran was nice, but she seemed suspicious when Thea didn't come. It was almost like she knew Thea was faking sick. After everything I had told Gran about her, maybe I should've known, too.

But this couldn't have worked out better if I had planned it myself.

"Ethan tells me you were a ballerina," Gran said to her.

"Yes, I trained in classical ballet. I spent a few summers here in the city as a teenager."

"Oh, lovely. Which ballet school did you attend?"

"The Humphrey School."

"Ah, yes. A bit of a way from here."

"Yes, I got really good at using the subway."

Gran laughed. "I haven't taken the subway in years."

Thea looked sideways at her, assessing Gran's extremely

expensive looking violet dress and jacket, paired with a violet hat and feathers. Gran loved to dress like Queen Elizabeth.

"I can't say I'm surprised," Thea said with a smile. "But it was the easiest and cheapest way to get around the city."

"Yes, I suppose that's true." She patted Thea's hand that was wrapped around her arm. "Would you like to feed the pigeons?"

"Oh, I...no, thank you," Thea responded.

"You should. It's quite miraculous. Feeding these creatures brings you closer to nature."

Thea looked back at me in alarm, and I bit the inside of my cheek to keep from bursting out in laughter. She protested, "I'm not really—"

"Nonsense," Gran insisted, grabbing a couple crusts of bread and shoving them into Thea's hands. "Hold your arms out and let the birds come to you. It's exhilarating."

If looks could kill, Thea's eyes would have stabbed me on the spot. But she acquiesced to Gran's request, slowly reaching her arms out.

"There!" Gran exclaimed. "Now wait."

Thea stood still for a few moments, and nothing happened. "Am I doing something wrong?"

"Patience!" Gran shouted.

Thea shut her mouth. I wished I could pull out my phone and take a picture of her, but then she'd *really* kill me.

Finally, a pigeon hopped over to Thea, tilting its head side to side, then flew up to her arm and took a piece of bread. Its feathers flapped around her arm, and she squealed, but the bird landed on her hand and peacefully ate the bread.

"No way," Thea breathed.

I smiled. She looked like a Disney princess, feeding the

birds and making friends with the forest creatures. Except we were, you know, in New York City.

Gran clapped her hands in delight. "You did it, my girl! Oh, look at all the birds coming now!"

"Wait, what?" Thea shrieked.

Did birds have some kind of silent call to alert each other about food? Because there were about fifty pigeons heading our way.

"Uh, Gran," I whispered. "Is this normal?"

"Not at all!" she replied. "Your Thea is something special."

Scratch that. Definitely needed to document this. I grabbed my phone and started recording a video.

Eyes wide in terror, Thea stood still with her arms outstretched as the flock landed around her feet and on her arms, eating the pieces of bread. She was frozen in place, looking around at the pigeons that started settling in her hair and pecking at her clothes.

"Okay, I think I'm done now!" she called. "How do I get them to go away?"

"The fun has just begun!" Gran called back.

"No, seriously," Thea said. "I'm really—oh, my goodness, *I think one of them just pooped on me!*"

Yikes. Time to put the phone away.

Thea's arms waved wildly around her head. "Shoo! Shoo birds! Get off!" She flung the crusts with all her might, and the birds flew away in search of the scattered pieces. I hurried over to her to assess the damage.

"Where did they poop on you?" I asked.

"In my hair," she wailed.

I walked around her and saw a giant white turd in the middle of her gorgeous red hair. "I do not envy you," I said.

"That doesn't help!" she said, smacking me on the arm. She peered around me to see Gran, who was cackling with glee. "Rita, I'm glad you're enjoying this, but I really need to get back to the hotel and wash my hair."

"Yes, yes, of course, dear," Gran replied. "Unfortunately, there's no quick way to walk out of the park."

Thea sighed. "Lead the way."

Gran turned back the other direction, Thea and I following along. Gran kept scattering the breadcrumbs as we walked, slowing her pace.

I nearly bumped into Gran. "Can we feed the pigeons again later? I think Thea would like to get back quickly."

"Oh, I'm sorry," Gran said, sounding completely unapologetic. "How about you two go on ahead? I'm slow, even when I'm not feeding the pigeons."

"You're okay alone?" I asked.

She patted my arm. "Ethan, my dear, I live here. This is my city. Don't worry about me. I'll see you later." And with a wink, she turned away from us and back to her pigeons.

Thea and I walked together in silence through the park.

"Do you know your way from here?" she asked.

"I do. I visit Gran every summer, and this is part of our morning routine. I know this part of Central Park like the back of my hand."

She nodded.

More silence.

Out of nowhere, she bolted off toward a water fountain and started filling her now-empty coffee cup with water. "I can't take this anymore. I can't be the girl who walked around Central Park with bird poop in her hair."

"And what exactly is your plan?" I asked.

"Can you pour this water over my head?" she asked. "At least this way, it will rinse out the bulk of it before we get to the hotel."

"Seriously?" I asked. No girl I knew would want water poured over their head in the middle of Central Park.

Then again, no girl I knew had been pooped on by a bird.

And no girl I knew was Thea.

"Yes, seriously," she snapped, handing me the cup. She sat down on the bench next to the fountain and leaned her head back, red hair cascading over the back of the bench. "Go."

This had to be one of the strangest encounters with a woman I'd ever had. But she demanded I clean her hair, so I was going to oblige.

I tipped the cup, water trickling, but it wasn't doing anything to move the giant white blob. Tipping the cup harder, the water gushed out a little too fast and splashed in Thea's face.

"Oh, my goodness," she said, wiping her eyes. "Are you kidding me right now?"

"I am so, so sorry," I said, trying to help wipe the rest off her face.

"Did you at least get it out?"

I glanced back at the turd, which was thankfully diluted by my deluge. "I think it's as good as it can get for now."

She nodded and pulled a hair tie out of her bag. "Ugh, I'll probably end up touching what's left of the poop, regardless." Her face twisted with disgust, then she lifted her arms and pulled her hair up high, getting ready to make a ponytail.

What was it about girls putting their hair up in a ponytail that was so attractive? Her hair was soaked, her face still dewy with moisture, but she was the most beautiful woman I had ever seen. I couldn't look away.

"You don't have to stare," she snapped.

"I'm not staring for the reasons you think I am," I replied.

She rolled her eyes. "There's no way you're about to hit on me when I have bird poop in my hair."

I gave her my signature half-smirk. "Nothing can hold me back when it comes to you."

She stood up quickly, marching past me to continue our trek. "You're insufferable," she muttered.

Eleven

THEA

As soon as we got back to the hotel, I bolted into my room to take a nice, long shower to wash bird poop and Ethan Taylor off of me. The problem was...I almost believed Ethan when he said he wasn't staring for a bad reason.

Did he *really* like me? Or was this all just a ploy? Was I this unreachable goal that he needed to achieve, or did he think there was actually something between us?

After my shower, I checked my phone and saw that Ethan had texted me.

> Hey. Quick note for the rest of the trip: if you don't want to hang out, you can just tell me. Don't lie about being sick.

Yeouch.

Technically, he wasn't wrong. But I didn't know what I

could or couldn't agree to on his itinerary. I needed space from him, and I didn't know how to ask.

My fingers hovered over the screen, trying to decide how to respond. Finally, I typed out my answer.

> Duly noted. Next time, I'll just tell you I don't want to be around you.

After sending it, I realized it sounded mean, when I meant to sound playful, so I sent an emoji face that was crossing its eyes and sticking out its tongue. There.

He didn't respond for the rest of the morning, and I thought I had hurt his feelings. But I took advantage of the alone time and scrolled through more TikTok sewing videos, distracting myself from the confusing mess I was putting myself in.

Around noon, a knock sounded on the adjoining door. I opened the door to find Ethan leaning against the doorway.

"Do you want to go get pizza or something?" he asked with a bit of hesitation.

I watched him for a moment, taking in a nervous Ethan. It was a look I wasn't accustomed to. He was almost… endearing.

"Sure," I finally said. "I'm starving."

His face brightened into a full grin, and I gestured to my front door.

"I'll meet you in the hallway," I said.

He nodded, and we closed our adjoining doors.

We walked in silence around the corner to the pizza shop. As soon as we stepped in the door, the smell of pizza overtook me and I nearly started drooling. That would be a great way to keep Ethan away from me. I perused the pizza through the windows, deciding which one I wanted.

"Ooh, they have white pie," I said.

"That's my favorite," Ethan said.

"Mine, too," I said, looking sideways at him. "But I always like to have another slice of something with red sauce to balance it out."

He smiled. "Perfect. Sounds like a good plan." He walked up to the counter and ordered a few slices for the two of us. I pulled out my wallet to pay my half, but Ethan put his hand on mine.

"I got it," he said.

I almost refused, so it wouldn't seem like a date, but Ivy's voice rang in my mind to take advantage of the opportunity and enjoy being treated to lunch.

We grabbed our slices and slid into a booth across from each other. Our knees brushed together, and I scooted over to the other side so I'd have some room. I didn't want any weird knee touching to confuse me more. The pizza filled me with glee, and I took a bite of the hot, cheesy goodness.

Ethan watched me carefully. "I have to admit, I'm surprised you wanted to eat pizza, with your ballet background and all."

I set my pizza down, taking a moment to decide how much I wanted to share. I studied his face, realizing that he wasn't saying anything to be judgmental. He seemed almost impressed.

"First of all," I began, "ballet burns a ton of calories. So I ate a lot when I was training. But you're right, I didn't eat a ton of pizza back then." I took a sip of soda.

"But now you're okay with it?" he asked.

I pursed my lips. "Well, I'm clearly not a ballerina," I said with a laugh, gesturing at my body. "When I turned sixteen, I developed some curves that are not really standard for ballerinas these days."

Ethan's eyes followed my hands, and he looked up with a wicked glint in his eyes. "I think I speak for men everywhere when I say that was a fortunate turn of events."

"Ugh, you pig." I rolled my eyes to hide the blush that crept up my cheeks. "Anyway, once I realized I couldn't pursue a career in ballet, I decided to enjoy myself and not worry about every imperfection. It's kind of hard to look at yourself objectively when you're in a room with mirrors for hours every single day. All you do in ballet is analyze the tiniest movement of your body, looking for the extra inch of rotation or holding your stomach in a little tighter, and it can be really hard to move away from that. But," I said, holding up my pizza, "I think I've struck a good balance now."

Ethan watched me take another bite, his face more serious than it had been all night. "I can relate to that."

"Oh, really?" I asked. "Did you take ballet growing up, too? I already know about the pageants."

His eyes widened. "No, you don't."

I laughed out loud. "Oh, I do. Your mom told Maritza Sanchez at the anniversary party last week."

He shook his head. "That was humiliating. At least it was short-lived." His eyes met mine again, back to his serious consideration. "But the pageants are part of it. Except that it's not my body or dancing on display. It's...me."

I tilted my head, not sure I understood what he meant.

He continued. "You had a mirror in the dance studio, right? Well, I have everyone around me, constantly judging my choices and my clothes and my career. I have a mirror held up to my entire life. I can handle it, and sometimes I enjoy it, but I see the way it's affected my mom."

"Your mom?" I asked, surprised that Ethan felt any kind of concern for his mother. "She seems like she loves being in the limelight."

"You talk about watching your weight for ballet. She watches her weight for television. Her entire life is broadcast for the entire nation." He shrugged, finally taking a bite of his pizza. "But I'm not sure that's much different from just being the wife of Nicholas Taylor. Besides, it was better than the alternative."

I raised a brow at him, but he didn't say more. What alternative did he mean? All this time, I'd mocked Rhonda Taylor and her obnoxious mannerisms, but I didn't think about what it would be like to be her. Having her every move watched. When she wasn't on camera, people were taking pictures of her, like they were of us in the airport. And even if she hadn't been on the show, her husband was well-known and influential in Orange County. No matter what, her life was on display, and she couldn't escape it.

"I'm sorry," I finally said. "I never thought about it that way."

He shrugged. "She's probably better for it. Doing the show gave her something to do."

"I mean for *you*," I said.

His eyes met mine in a rare, serious moment. He opened his mouth to say something, then closed it. His eyes darted around the restaurant, and a big smile lit his face. "Well, I'd say I turned out just fine, don't you think?"

I shook my head and sighed. So close.

We finished our food and stepped out of the restaurant onto the street. As if we were on a movie set and someone called the special effects guy, it started raining.

Scratch that. Pouring.

I had no umbrella, and not even a jacket to cover me. Just my purse and a thin cotton dress. Fabulous. I took off running, and Ethan followed along, laughing the whole way.

My foot slipped on the sidewalk, and I went down. With my face an inch from the pavement, Ethan's steady hands grabbed my waist from behind and pulled me back up to standing. He held me flush against the front of his body, steadying me. The heat from his body wrapped around mine, and I felt a little weak in the knees.

Because I almost fell, right?

Right.

"Are you okay?" he asked.

For the second time today, water coursed over my face, but I didn't want to move. I tried to say, *yes, I'm fine,* but I felt like I swallowed my tongue and made a weird clicking noise instead. I cleared my throat. "Yep."

He squeezed my waist once, then stepped away from me. My mind cleared, and I remembered I was wearing a super thin dress and needed to get out of this rain ASAP. I started running (more carefully this time), and soon Ethan and I were back at the hotel.

We stepped inside, and waves of shame crashed into me. *Of course,* I would walk into this swanky hotel looking like a wet rat. I didn't belong here. Ethan still looked like a model, his clothes sticking to his body and accentuating his physique. Laughing and smiling, he ran a hand through his wet hair and shook out the rain. "Come on," he said, leading me to the elevator with a hand on the small of my back.

The elevator doors shut, and I got a good look at my reflection in the gold-framed mirrors. "Oh, my goodness," I said, wiping the mascara that smudged under my eyes. "I look crazy."

"You look perfect."

I turned my head to look at Ethan, expecting a flirty grin or a smug wink. Instead, I met eyes deep with intensity, drinking me in.

No one had looked at me like that.

Not even Stefan, and we were engaged.

He held me captive, and I couldn't look away. Slowly, he raised his hand to my face and used his thumb to gently wipe under my eye. His fingers lingered on my cheek, sending a shiver down my spine.

But in an instant, he switched back to his usual self. "Sorry, no flirting," he said, holding his hands up in surrender and giving me a wink.

"Yeah, right," I said. "Don't forget it." My voice was so shaky, but I turned back to the mirror and hoped he wouldn't notice.

We arrived at our floor and walked in silence to our rooms. He stopped in front of my door as I fumbled for my key.

"We don't have to do anything else today," he said. "So, I'll see you in the morning."

I didn't respond. I didn't know how to explain that I wanted to spend more time with him, but needed to stay as far away from him as possible. As far as I could while being next door to him. With an adjoining hotel room door.

He cleared his throat at my silence. "We have breakfast with Gran at nine. Just knock on the adjoining door when you're ready."

I nodded. I was too confused to speak clearly. My mouth couldn't be trusted right now because my head was a muddled mess. I opened the door and stepped inside my room, pressing my back against the door. What was happening? Why was Ethan Taylor starting to seem like...a real person? It was so much easier when I could hate him from afar. But now...now I didn't know what to think anymore.

Twelve

THEA

After taking my second shower of the day (because I couldn't trust the rain in Manhattan to be clean), I decided to check in with my mom and Ivy. I shot a text to my mom.

> Hey Mama. Everything's going well here in NYC! Got pooped on by a pigeon and caught in a rainstorm. But the pizza is delicious, and I'll have more to report tomorrow.

Then I sent a message to Ivy.

> Hey girl! Hope all is well at the studio. NYC has been great so far (except Ethan blech).

I had to ask myself if I really felt that way. Was Ethan still "blech"?

I refused to think too hard about it.

Ivy wrote back first, as usual.

I loved her message and left it at that. I wasn't ready to explain anything else to her, like how his touch set me on fire and there were glimpses of an Ethan that I didn't hate.

Instead of texting me back, my mom called. "Hey, Mama," I said, answering the phone.

"Sounds like you're having an eventful day," she said, a smile in her voice.

"You could say that," I replied. "But it hasn't been all bad."

"Is Ethan driving you crazy?" she asked.

I was about to say *yes, of course*, but I stopped myself. Was he? It was more like he was confusing me than driving me crazy.

"Oh, hesitation," my mom murmured.

I groaned. "I don't know what I think."

"Don't think so hard. Just enjoy yourself."

"Easy for you to say." I sighed, flopping down on my bed. "How's Miles?"

"He's good. Keeping busy with all his programming. He entered a robot building competition, so he's staying up a little too late working on it every night. But I'd rather he work on that than something else."

"You and Dad taught us to work hard. It's in our blood."

"I guess so. But maybe we should have taught you to have more fun. What are you doing tonight?"

I twisted my lips to the side, realizing I had no plans. "Ethan said we had nothing this evening, but staying in my room feels like a waste."

"Yes, it is! You're in Manhattan! What do you want to do?"

I pulled out my itinerary and looked through our plans for the rest of the week. A few family meals were planned, but not much else. "I wonder if I could go see a show," I said.

"That's perfect! You can check if any shows have an extra seat. If you're by yourself, that will be easier."

My mind started racing through the plans I needed to make, and excitement pulsed through my veins. "Okay, I'm going to do it!"

"Great, love bug. Have an awesome time. Tell me all about it tonight."

"Will do. Thank you, Mama. I love you."

"Love you too. Have fun."

We hung up, and I excitedly raced around my room, getting a new outfit together for an evening on the town. There was a subway station right near the hotel, and I was sure my memory of how to navigate the subway system would come back to me. This would be a great night.

THE NEXT MORNING, I was sitting on my giant fluffy bed and checked my watch for the fifteenth time.

"Are you ready yet?" I called through the adjoining door. We were supposed to be at his grandmother's apartment in ten minutes, and he still wasn't ready.

"Perfection like this takes time," Ethan called back.

I rolled my eyes, even though he couldn't see. "Perfection is relative," I replied.

He laughed. "I'm decent. My door is unlocked. You can come in now."

Finally. I'd been waiting in my room for over twenty minutes, scrolling through TikTok, watching super cool sped-up sewing progress videos, but even that had grown stale. While I was glad to have my own room, it was starting to feel like a prison.

I stepped into his room for a sight I wasn't prepared for: Ethan Taylor, shirtless, with dress slacks.

"You...I..." I couldn't find the words. "This is not decent!" I exclaimed.

"What are you talking about? You'd see less than this at the beach," he said.

"No flirting!" I shouted as I ran back into my room.

"I wasn't flirting!" he called back with a laugh. "Unless you see something here that you want..."

"Nope! I'm good! I'll come back when you're *fully* dressed, thank you very much!" I flopped on my bed and fanned myself. *Perfection* was right. Curse Ethan Taylor. How was I going to stay next door to him now knowing that all *that* was under his shirt? His body was perfect. Rounded shoulders, sculpted abs, biceps that were just right. I had to keep reminding myself of his personality and the time I slapped him in the face. Maybe we had fun yesterday afternoon getting pizza, but that wasn't the real him. That was Ethan without all his people around.

Right?

I was so shaken up, I actually tidied my room. Apparently all I needed to start cleaning was to be startled by a handsome man with perfect muscles.

"Okay, I'm *fully* dressed now," he called.

I took a deep breath and smoothed my dress. It was a deep green, cap-sleeved, fitted cocktail dress with cream heels I figured was appropriate for breakfast with the famous "Gran." But I knew Ethan would tell me if I was wrong.

I stepped into his room and breathed a sigh of relief that Ethan was fully dressed. A navy-blue suit, light-blue dress shirt, but no tie. His hair was neatly in place, and he was freshly shaved. I had to admit, I preferred the bit of stubble he had yesterday afternoon. Either way, though, it really felt like he stepped right off the Dior runway.

"How's my outfit?" I asked, doing a little twirl for him.

"Perfect," he said with a smile.

"See?" I replied. "I told you that you could trust my judgment."

His face sobered. After a moment of hesitation, he said, "Thank you."

I furrowed my brow. "For what?" I asked.

"Being considerate of my weird obsession with proper attire."

"At least you're admitting that it's weird," I retorted with a smile. "But now that I understand where it came from, I guess I kind of get it."

"Thank you for that," he said, locking eyes with me. "You're right. I should have believed you." The moment felt charged, electricity passing between us. It wasn't just my understanding of his obsession. He had shared a piece of his history that led to one of his weird habits, and I understood.

I didn't want to dwell on it. "We'd better go, right?" I asked.

He checked his watch. "Yes, you're right. Let's head out." He held the door open for me and we walked to the elevator. But instead of pushing the down button, he pushed up.

"Wait, where are we going?" I asked.

"To the penthouse. That's where Gran lives."

"Your grandmother lives in the penthouse of this hotel?" He shrugged.

"Awesome," I breathed. As much as I disliked these people, I loved seeing and experiencing life through their eyes.

Ethan offered me his hand, a reminder of the charade we needed to play in front of his grandmother. I slowly placed my hand in his, and again felt that connection I wished I didn't. We arrived at the top floor, and the elevator doors opened to a foyer with a security guard.

"Hey, Roger," Ethan said to the guard. Roger didn't acknowledge him, just pressed the button to open the sliding door behind him.

"Always a pleasure," Ethan said, saluting him. "He's a big softie," he whispered to me. I caught Roger rolling his eyes as we walked past and couldn't help the snort that emerged.

We walked into the apartment, and I thought I was walking into a museum. Sofas that looked like they belonged in the palace of Versailles, statues of children and birds. Birds everywhere. Statues, figurines, paintings, everything had birds on them. No wonder Rita loved feeding the pigeons.

She was waiting for us on one of the stiff couches, wearing a royal-blue suit jacket and a dress with a matching hat.

"Ethan, Thea! So glad to see you both," she said, standing up to hug us.

"Gran, you don't have to get up," Ethan said.

"Nonsense," she said, swatting his arm. "Like you said, I'm not dying."

He smirked and wrapped her in a big hug. Without the fear of being caught in my "sick in bed" lie, I could observe their interaction. She only came up to his shoulder, but it was clear she was in control.

Rita pulled away from Ethan and took my hand in her warm, soft one.

"Thea, darling, you look lovely," she said.

"Oh, thank you. Your royal blue suits you."

She beamed and smoothed her dress, gesturing for us to sit with her. Ethan settled back in his chair, crossing one ankle over his knee in the way men do, but the smile on his face showed how joyful he was to be here.

"So, how was your day after the pigeons?" Rita asked.

"Not bad," Ethan said. "We ate pizza and then got caught in the rain."

"Oh, how romantic!" Rita said, clapping her hands.

"It was," Ethan agreed, looking over at me with a soft smile.

I wished he wasn't right.

"What else?" Rita asked.

Ethan looked over at me, unsure of my evening plans.

"I saw Hamilton," I offered.

Rita and Ethan both turned to me with matching round eyes. The family resemblance was a little startling.

"Without Ethan?" Rita asked slowly.

I realized my error. We were supposed to be *dating*, and I had a solo adventure last night.

"Uh, yes," Ethan said, stepping in for me. "I was exhausted and jet lagged, so I told her to go out if she wanted to."

"Jet lagged," Rita repeated. "When your time zone is behind ours."

I giggled nervously, about to say something stupid. Thankfully, Rita's maid scooted over to the sitting area and informed us that breakfast was ready.

I'm so sorry, I mouthed to Ethan. He made a gesture of wiping his forehead in relief, but he didn't seem too upset.

We sat down at the gigantic dining room table and started eating the most incredible eggs benedict I had ever tasted.

"So, Thea," Rita said. "Tell me how you and Ethan met."

I blinked, a deer in headlights. Why hadn't we prepared this part of the story? Ethan shrugged at me.

Should I just tell her the truth?

Why the heck not?

"Well, it's a funny story. I actually wasn't a big fan of Ethan's when we first met."

"Oh?" Rita asked, politely taking a bite.

"Yes. He made some inappropriate comments. So I slapped him in the face."

Rita choked. After taking a sip of water to clear her throat, she said, "I see."

Ethan smiled. "I won't deny it. She was completely in the right."

I tilted my head at him. Did he really think that? Or was he just acting for his grandmother?

"When was this, exactly?" Rita asked.

"A little over a year ago," I answered.

She narrowed her eyes, assessing us both. Her expression relaxed, and she took another dainty bite. "That makes sense. I've seen a bit of growth in Ethan over the last year."

"Oh?" I asked, then internally kicked myself for acting so surprised.

"Yes. I always thought it was his friendship with Amethyst King that changed his attitude, but I'm sure you had a part in it as well."

I turned my head to look directly at Ethan. His eyes met mine with a startling openness and sincerity. It was true: Ethan from one year ago seemed like a different person than the Ethan in front of me, having breakfast with his grandmother. But I couldn't reconcile the two in my mind, no matter how hard I tried.

"Do you have any plans tonight?" Rita asked suddenly.

I looked over at Ethan for confirmation, who shook his head.

Rita hopped up and scurried into the kitchen.

"Where is she going?" I asked.

"You never know with Gran," he said, taking another bite of his breakfast.

"Am I doing okay?" I whispered, taking advantage of the moment alone.

Ethan raised a brow.

"At pretending we're dating."

"Oh." He dabbed his mouth with his napkin. "Well, you did complicate things by going to Hamilton alone. I'm sure she could use a little more convincing."

I guessed he was right. I put my hand on his, faking a laugh as Rita reemerged with an envelope.

"Oh, I hope I'm not interrupting anything!" Rita said with a glint in her eye.

"Nothing that can't be resumed," Ethan said with a wicked smile.

"How disappointing." She handed the envelope to Ethan. "Here. I have two tickets to Lincoln Center tonight that I won't be using. It's for a ballet. I don't know which one."

"Oh, no, we couldn't!" I exclaimed.

She waved her hand at me. "An old lady like me can't stay awake that late."

Ethan opened the envelope and read the tickets out loud. "The Royal Ballet presents Cinderella." He raised his eyes to meet mine. "Box seats, too."

My heart rose into my throat. My favorite ballet company performing my favorite ballet. This had to be a joke.

"I also know a couple people who work there," Rita added casually. "I could make a phone call, and you could go backstage after the show to look at the costumes."

This was a dream come true. Minus Ethan, of course. But if it wasn't for him, this opportunity wouldn't exist.

"What do you say, Thea?" Ethan asked, bringing me out of my daze.

I blinked a few times. Even though it meant a full evening with Ethan, how could I say no?

"Yes! Oh, thank you Rita!" I jumped out of my seat, squeezing her in a hug.

She chuckled. "You're welcome, my dear." With a wink at Ethan, she turned back to her breakfast.

My mind whirled, planning outfits and shoe combinations. I truly felt like Cinderella going to the ball. I glanced over at Ethan, who watched me and seemed energized by my enthusiasm. If only my Prince Charming didn't have an ego the size of a pumpkin carriage, this would be my personal fairy tale.

Thirteen

ETHAN

I missed Thea. Already.

She spent the afternoon shopping for fabric. We hadn't spent any time together over the last year that I had known her, and already I missed her presence. I loved that she called me out on my crap and didn't let me get away with any of my "smarminess," as she called it. After being lonely for such a long time, I was startled by how perfectly we matched together.

But I had to be careful. If I took things too fast, she'd run away. Or slap me in the face again. It was best to protect myself, which meant giving her the smallest hints and touches without scaring her off.

We had agreed to get dinner separately, so I grabbed some food from the street vendors before heading back to the room to get ready. I heard her door open and shut loudly.

"We're leaving in thirty minutes," I called into her room.

"Yeah, yeah," she shouted back.

Thirty-two minutes later, I paced nervously in my room, waiting for her. Loud rock music blared through the door. Was that really her music of choice?

"Are you almost done?" I shouted, hoping she would hear me.

"Perfection takes time," she called back, echoing my words from yesterday. I laughed out loud, thankful for her lightening my tense mood.

Finally, the music turned off. Her door opened and a pair of golden strappy stilettos stepped into my room. I followed the line of her dancer legs to an adorable, golden yellow tulle skirt paired with a solid black fitted tank top. She wore a gold necklace and had pulled her red hair into a high bun. She fit the part of the ballerina on a night on the town.

My breath caught in my throat. I finally looked at her eyes, which were watching my observation. "What do you think?" she asked.

"You're perfect," I said. We stared at each other for a moment, the air hanging thick around us. I cleared my throat. "It was well worth the wait."

"I'm glad you approve of my attire," she quipped. I lifted the corner of my mouth into a grin.

"Let me grab my bag," she said, turning back into her room. Mindlessly, I followed her, forgetting all about the rules and staying out of her personal space. But the sight that greeted me pulled me from my stupor.

"What happened in here?" I exclaimed.

She whipped around, her cheeks red. "You weren't supposed to see my room!"

It looked like a burglar had ransacked her room. Clothes

were *everywhere.* Makeup littered the vanity. There were five pairs of shoes on her bed.

"Is that..." I pointed up at the post of her bed, where something pink and lacy was hanging.

Thea squeaked out loud and snatched what I can only assume was a pair of her undergarments. "I *told* you not to be here!"

I backed out of the room slowly, my hands raised in surrender. "I think if I stay any longer, I'll get lost in the tornado."

She put her hands on my chest and shoved me out. "Do *not* come in here again."

"Auntie Em! Toto!" I called, quoting Dorothy.

"Out!" She rolled her eyes, grabbed her golden handbag on the vanity, and pulled me by the hand out of the room. She must not have realized our hands were joined until we reached the hallway of the hotel, where she quickly dropped my hand like it was on fire.

She cleared her throat and smoothed down her skirt. "I'm glad you like the outfit," she said softly, betraying how much my opinion actually *did* matter to her. Interesting.

"It's perfect. I promise." I wished I could slide my hand around her waist and give her a light kiss on the cheek to show her what I thought, but I didn't have an excuse for that. Not yet. I'd find my moment later tonight.

We headed down the elevator, where Hayk waited for us next to the car. Once we were settled in our seats, I cleared my throat. "I have to ask—"

"Yes, I've always been this messy, and no, I don't foresee any change."

"Not that," I said, laughing. "Your music."

"What about it?"

"I thought ballerinas were into classical music."

She wrinkled her nose. "Not for fun. Classical music is fine, and I enjoy dancing to it, but that's not what I listen to in my car."

"Or when you're getting dressed."

She shrugged. "Sometimes you gotta rock out."

A vision of Thea with dark eyeliner moshing at a concert made me smile. "Who's your favorite band?"

She twisted her lips to the side. "That's tricky. But probably Fall Out Boy. The lead singer even did the theme song for a kids' Spiderman show, and it's pretty awesome."

"I'll have to check it out sometime."

A small smile played on her lips, light in her eyes. But she looked out the window a moment later, effectively ending the conversation.

"Have you seen Cinderella before?" I asked, wanting to draw her attention back to me.

Her face lit with excitement. "Only once. But I performed it with my studio when I was fifteen."

"Oh, really?"

She nodded. "My studio always performed a classic ballet in the spring. Sleeping Beauty, Le Corsaire, Coppelia. When I was fifteen, my teacher chose Cinderella. I was the fairy godmother." She giggled and gazed into the distance. "I caught a nasty cold the week of the performance, though."

"That stinks. Did you have to stay home?"

She shook her head. "That wasn't an option. There was no understudy. So I took a ton of DayQuil and was a crazy hyper mess, but I didn't feel sick and got to perform."

My lips twisted into a grin. "That doesn't surprise me."

She furrowed her brow. "What does that mean?"

I shrugged my shoulders. "You're determined to work hard and follow through on your commitments. You have goals and you want to reach them. Even if you're super sick."

She blinked at me, watching me carefully.

I cleared my throat. "What is it?"

She bit her lip. "I guess I didn't think you knew much about me. Or that you saw anything about me beyond the surface."

I held her gaze a moment more. "I see you, Thea." And I really, really liked what I saw. But that was probably too much, too soon.

The air was charged around us, neither of us wanting to break eye contact. The car door opened, startling us both. "We're here," Hayk said. He looked back and forth between us, a big smile spreading on his face.

Thea broke out of her stupor and took Hayk's hand, exiting the car. That moment was a major win. I knew I was breaking through. But I had to be careful. I stepped out behind her, and Hayk squeezed my shoulder.

"You picked a good one," he whispered to me.

I know.

We headed into Lincoln Center with about ten minutes to spare. I let Thea lead me around, exploring the different floors and sights. The bells chimed, letting us know the show was about to start, and we headed to our box seats.

"Oh, this is perfect," Thea breathed.

The glow in her cheeks and the light in her eyes were thrilling to watch. I took advantage of her excitement to ask her some more questions. "So, did you dance on toe?"

Her expression changed so quickly from delight to disgust. "On what?"

"You know…" I mimicked dancing on my toes with my hands pointed down. "With toe shoes."

A few of the people in the box with us shot me judgmental glances.

"What did I say wrong?" I asked.

Thea shook her head. "For someone who claims to be so cultured, you really don't know anything about ballet."

"I never claimed to know anything about ballet."

"Have you seen one before?"

"Just one, when I was thirteen. Sleeping Beauty. It was so boring. All I wanted to do was go home and play video games."

"Video games, huh?" she asked. "Like what?"

"StarCraft," I replied.

Her eyes widened. "That's my brother's favorite game."

"How old is your brother?" I asked.

"He's fourteen. But he's a huge nerd, unlike you."

I pictured a fourteen-year-old version of Thea and smiled. "I'd love to meet him," I replied.

She blinked a few times in surprise. Clearing her throat, she turned the conversation back to the ballet. "The middle of Sleeping Beauty drags a bit. But the *pas de deux* is so gorgeous."

"Wait, do you speak French?" I asked.

She rolled her eyes. "I can't believe I have to explain this. All ballet terms are in French. *Pas de deux* means 'dance of two.' And the correct term for dancing 'on toe' is *en pointe*."

I held my hands up in surrender. "Excuse me. So did you dance *en pointe*?"

"Haven't you noticed my deformed toes?" she asked with a laugh. "Of course I did."

I bent down to look at her toes in her gold shoes. "Sheesh, girl! Do all ballerinas' toes look like that?"

"Not all," she replied. She bent down with me and squished her toes together, fitting like puzzle pieces. "My toes are really bony, and I went *en pointe* a little younger than I should have. So my bones developed a little oddly. Some people have more squishy toes, which actually gives them a little extra cushion."

I sat back up, slightly grossed out. "That's weird."

"Well, thanks," she said sarcastically, straightening up as well. "I never thought I'd see the day where I'd turn you off."

Shoot. This was going the wrong direction. "Thankfully, I couldn't care less about your toes. They're my least favorite part of the human anatomy, so your weird toes don't affect the way I see you."

She opened her mouth to reply, but the lights went down and cut off her inevitable snarky reply. Or a reminder to stop flirting. It was better this way.

Melancholic notes wafted through the theater, signaling the beginning of the show, and we settled into our seats. The curtain rose on Cinderella fixing her stepsisters' skirts, who were played by men and highly entertaining. The first act took place entirely in Cinderella's home, following the stepsisters getting ready for the ball and a dance lesson by an instructor. I kept up with the story without checking the program, which said something about this ballet.

I kept sneaking glances over at Thea. She was enthralled. If I thought she was beautiful before, now she was enchanting. Stunning. Her eyes lit with delight, a light smile fixed on her lips.

When the fairy godmother appeared, I nudged her elbow with mine. "There you are," I whispered. "Do you think she's on DayQuil, too?"

She turned her head to me and smiled. I loved our little secret. The fairies danced, Cinderella got her gown and carriage, and she headed off to the ball.

The lights flickered on for intermission, and everyone stood. "Do you want to get some champagne?" I asked.

She blinked a few times, deciding. She seemed unsure, maybe wondering if she wanted to let her guard down around me. I didn't want to push her into anything she wasn't ready for, so I waited patiently. "Sure," she finally agreed. "But I need to use the restroom. I'll meet you out in the lobby."

We walked out the door and parted ways. I waited in the long line for refreshments, killing time by messing around on my phone. Halfway to the counter, a tap on my shoulder brought me back to the moment. I turned my head to the person behind me in line and found a blonde bombshell in a skin-tight dress and sky-high heels, batting her lashes at me.

"Hello," she purred. "Why is a handsome guy like you here at the ballet?"

Out of the corner of my eye, I glimpsed Thea in her golden skirt. I pointed at her across the way. "Taking that gorgeous girl to see her favorite company in the world."

The blonde's eyes darted over to Thea walking toward us, and a thin smile pressed on her lips. She took a tiny step back and murmured, "Enjoy your evening."

I nodded my head at her, then smiled widely at Thea. She

had slowed her steps, seeing me talking to the girl behind me, but picked up her speed when she saw my face.

Knowing that I had to make a bit of a gesture to prove something to the woman, I took advantage and slid my hand around her waist, pulling her close to me. "Hey, babe," I said, kissing her on the head.

Instead of pulling away, like she did with Stefan and Tabitha, she leaned into me. "Hey. I guess the line was longer than you expected."

"It's fine. Now I have company."

She tilted her head up to me and smiled, her eyes flicking back to the woman behind us in line. I shrugged, trying to convey that it meant nothing.

A year ago, I would have bought that woman a drink and spent the evening trying to flirt with her (and probably trying to sneak out early). Now, all I wanted was to spend time with Thea. I didn't notice other women, because there was only her.

And it seemed like she understood. I reveled in being this close to her, holding her in my arms, knowing that she wasn't running away. I'd take advantage of this time when she was willing to pretend, even for a moment, that something burned between us. We got our drinks, and I knew I had to capitalize on this. I just had to find my moment.

Fourteen

ETHAN

We took our seats after drinking our champagne with a few minutes left of intermission. Thea finally asked, "What was with the woman in line?"

I shrugged. "She was hitting on me."

She huffed a laugh. "You say it so casually."

"I'm not going to lie about it."

"Ah, there's the modest Ethan Taylor we all know."

Now it was my turn to huff a laugh. "Modest and Ethan Taylor don't normally go together." I sat back in my seat. "But I told her I was here with you. Thank you for going along with it."

She kept her eyes on me. "I was a little surprised you weren't interested. She seemed like your type."

"Oh, really?" I asked. "How do you know my type?"

"I've seen you at all the events. Tall and blonde with a skin-tight dress is usually your thing."

I trained my eyes on her, holding her gaze for a moment. "I'm not interested in that anymore."

A flush rose in her cheeks. She seemed a little stunned, but the lights went down and the music began, preventing her from saying more.

The second act opened at the ball. I wouldn't lie; the beginning was a little boring. It was a bunch of courtiers dancing around. But I took advantage of the less-interesting performance to watch Thea. Her eyes twinkled, and she drank in every moment. A thrill ran through me, knowing I had given her this evening and opportunity. Technically Gran did, but I was the reason we were in New York at all.

The music changed, ethereal with twinkling bells, and Thea's breath caught. It must have been time for Cinderella's grand entrance. I looked to the stage, watching the fairies entering the ball and hopping around. The moment Cinderella came on stage, Thea whispered, "Oh, wow."

Her eyes were wide, a smile lighting her face, and her breathing was shallow. On stage, Cinderella took the prince's hand, and he began leading her down the stairs while she took each step on her toes (I was sure there was another French technical term for that, but I didn't know what it was.)

It was now or never. Thea's hands were resting on her lap. Slowly, keeping my face toward the stage but my eyes on my target, I reached my hand toward hers and lightly brushed my fingers over the top of her hand. I closed my fingers around her soft, dainty ones, waiting to see what she would do. Would she implement the "no flirting" rule? Or would she go along with the moment?

She kept her eyes on the stage, pretending she didn't notice anything happening. Cinderella kept descending the giant staircase, her hand in the prince's. Finally, Thea turned her hand over and wrapped her fingers around my hand in return.

I exhaled the breath I didn't know I had been holding and settled back in my chair. When was the last time I wanted to hold hands? Was I twelve years old again? But this thrill, knowing that she trusted me enough to hold my hand willingly, knowing who I was and what had happened between us, made my heart race like nothing I had experienced in the last year. I was breaking down the barrier between us.

WE SPENT the rest of the act holding hands. During the next intermission, we walked around the lobby arm in arm. Thea never brought up the change in our physical situation, and I didn't want to scare her off by saying anything, either. We pretended this was normal for us. And when we sat down for the final act of the show, I confidently reached over for her hand, and she immediately squeezed mine back.

It was working.

After the show, we headed backstage and met the costume designer, just like Gran had promised. Thea was in awe of the tutus and dresses, reverently touching each one and asking all the questions the designer wanted to hear. He was thrilled to speak "costume design" with someone who knew what she was talking about, and Thea was as enchanting as ever. I was proud to watch her in her element, and impressed she was making such a great impression on someone who was at the top of his game.

We finally wandered outside around midnight, hand in hand, and I texted Hayk that we were ready to be picked up.

"He said he'll be here in about five minutes," I reported.

Thea nodded. The lights illuminated her green eyes and made the gold in her outfit sparkle. I couldn't imagine anyone looking more angelic.

"Did you enjoy your evening?" I asked.

She nodded, a small smile on her lips. "It was…better than I ever anticipated."

"I'm glad." I smiled back at her, taking advantage of the intimacy of the night to hold her gaze.

"Thank you," she said.

I raised an eyebrow. "For?"

"A great evening."

I shrugged. "You should thank Gran, not me."

"Ethan Taylor, not taking praise when offered to him?" she challenged, her eyes teasing with laughter.

I sighed dramatically. "I am so sorry. What a lapse."

She laughed out loud. "But I don't just mean the ballet. I mean the whole night. And the whole trip." We were already standing close together, holding hands, but she took a tiny step even closer. "These few days have been…not what I imagined."

My heart started racing. "How so?" I asked, keeping my voice calm.

She bit her bottom lip. I couldn't help it; my eyes flicked down to her perfect mouth, then back to her eyes.

I tried my best to be patient. I really did. But I held back all night, and I was reaching my limit.

So instead of waiting for an answer, I started leaning my face toward hers. Slowly, slowly, giving her the chance to pull away and tell me I was reading every signal wrong.

She didn't.

She leaned toward me, lips parting, eyes closing, her breath on mine, and then—

HONK!!!!!

Startled, we jumped away from each other.

"What the—" I started.

"Hello, you two!" Hayk called through the open window. He exited the car and opened the back door. "Did you have a good night?"

I sighed. Seriously, that was not cool.

"Yes, thank you!" Thea answered for us, letting go of my hand and climbing into the car.

I glared at Hayk, and he winked at me. Even though I loved him like an uncle, family disagreed sometimes. I climbed in behind Thea, hoping I'd get some kind of sign that she wasn't mortified over our almost-kiss. Hayk closed the door and got back into the driver's seat.

"How was the ballet?" he asked.

"Incredible," Thea said. She glanced over at me. "One of the best nights I've had in a long time."

Yes, yes, yes. I held her gaze, my chest warming.

"Wonderful," Hayk said. "Am I taking you back to the hotel?"

"Is that what you want?" I asked her.

Keeping her eyes on mine, she opened her mouth once and shut it. "Not yet," she finally said.

"How about some dessert? I know just the place," Hayk said, glancing over his shoulder at the traffic.

She *wanted* to spend more time with me. One more point.

Thea pulled out her phone. "I haven't checked it all night," she said apologetically. "I'll be quick."

I shook my head. "I've been on my phone plenty of times around you. No worries."

She tapped a few things, then her face fell. "Oh, no," she murmured, putting her hand over her mouth.

"What's wrong?" I asked.

"It's Ivy. She said Adalynn twisted something in her knee." The car jolted forward, and Thea typed out a response. Setting the phone in her lap, she rubbed her forehead, her eyes squeezing. She looked like she was in pain. Was the champagne already giving her a headache? She only had one glass.

"Who's Adalynn?" I asked.

"She's one of our teen dancers. She's incredible, and this was going to be her last season before graduation. We had a beautiful solo planned for her." Her phone buzzed, and she picked it up again. "Ivy says she has to get an MRI, but they think it's serious." With one hand on her forehead, Thea typed out another response to Ivy. I could tell she was upset, but I had no clue what to say or do to help.

"I'm sorry. That's awful."

She nodded, continuing to type her message. A minute later, she squeezed her eyes shut. "Oh, shoot."

"What now?" I asked.

Her eyes stayed pinched shut in pain. "I get severe motion sickness. This is why I never text in a moving car."

"Oh. What...what do you need?" I gently reached my hand over and placed it on top of hers.

"Um...I need..." She took in a deep breath. "We need to go back to the hotel. Sorry."

I squeezed her hand. "Not a problem." I leaned forward and relayed the message to Hayk.

"Normally I'd ask to open the windows, but Manhattan isn't known for its fresh air," she said, her eyes still shut. She squeezed my hand tightly, then pressed her other hand to her mouth. After a few moments, she pulled it back down. "I'm sorry. This is so embarrassing."

"Don't be embarrassed," I said, rubbing the top of her hand. "We'll get you back and you'll be able to rest."

She nodded, her face scrunched in pain. I had heard of people with motion sickness problems like this, but I had never experienced it myself. I wasn't sure what would help or make it worse, so I stayed quiet and held her hand.

Within a few minutes, Hayk had us back at the hotel. I held her hand to help her out of the car, then tucked her into my side so she could lean on me. Hayk rubbed her shoulder sympathetically and gave me a sad smile.

"Thanks, Hayk," I said. "We'll see you tomorrow."

He got back in the car and drove off, and Thea leaned on me as we walked into the hotel. In the elevator, she rested all her weight on me, and when we got to our floor, I scooped her up and carried her down the hallway.

"This is so embarrassing," she murmured, but she didn't fight it and nestled her head into my chest. I hated that the reason we were so close was because she felt awful, but having her rest on me stirred up more emotions than any contact I'd had with any other woman.

I set her down to open the door to her room. As soon as the door was open, I scooped her up again. She rested back in my arms, and I carried her inside.

"You just had to leave this crazy mess on your bed, huh?" I asked with a chuckle. I set her down on the edge of the bed, the one sliver of space to fit her body. Once she was lying down, I grabbed all the clothes surrounding her in an enormous pile and dumped them on the side. That wasn't important right now. I walked back and knelt next to her.

"What do you need?" I asked.

She groaned. "My head is killing me. I need to lie here and never get up." She paused. "And a bowl. I might need to throw up."

That got me moving. I rushed around the room, settling on the ice bucket, and brought it over to her bed. "It's on the floor if you need it."

"Thank you," she murmured. Her eyes were still pinched shut. Her head must have been killing her. I figured her hair being pulled back didn't help with that, so I reached behind her head and started fiddling with the pins.

"What are you doing?" she murmured.

"Trying to take out your hair." I found the little metallic pins, pulled them out, then gently pulled the rubber band holding her hair together. My fingers gently dug into her scalp, and her small moan let me know I was helping.

"Thank you," she said again. "You don't have to do this."

"I know." I continued my ministrations. "What else can I do? Take off your shoes?"

"Sure," she said, huffing a laugh. "Ethan Taylor taking off my shoes. What is happening in the world?"

I smirked. I was winning her over, that's what was

happening. Unbuckling the straps of her shoes, I took them off and gave her feet a small little rub. But I wasn't about to spend a ton of time around her weird toes. Besides, I knew that her head caused her pain, so I went back to the top of the bed and started rubbing her head again.

"That feels amazing. Thank you."

"You don't have to keep thanking me."

Her eyes finally fluttered open, their green depths pulling into my soul. "I mean it."

"You're welcome." I looked down at her body, noticing her skirt all around her legs. "I could help you out of your skirt, too," I joked.

She smacked me on the back of my head. "Still the same Ethan Taylor."

"Hopefully not exactly the same."

She smiled at me, melting me a little more. "Not the same. Not what I expected."

Yes.

She settled back into her pillow, closing her eyes again. "When I was little and got motion sickness, my dad would rub my head and tell me a story."

Her dad. My heart ached for her. If I could do one small thing to ease her pain, I would. "What kind of stories would he tell you?"

"Mostly stories about Barbie and Ken. He'd make up silly stories about them going on adventures together."

I smirked. "You know, I've been compared to Ken before."

"No kidding," she muttered. I couldn't tell if that was good or bad.

"I can tell you a story," I offered.

"Really?"

"Oh, yes. I'm a master storyteller." Not really. But I could fake it.

She opened her eyes, moisture gathering. "That would be really nice."

I started stroking her hair. "Once upon a time, Barbie and Ken took a trip to New York..."

Fifteen

THEA

My eyes blinked blearily, and I immediately noticed my headache was gone. I breathed a sigh of relief, settling into my pillow. Thankfully, I never threw up, but that headache was one of the worst I'd had in a while. I fluttered my eyes open and found Ethan Taylor asleep on the floor below me.

Panic set in. I sucked in a quiet breath. *Think, Thea, think. How did this happen?* I remembered him telling me a ridiculous story about Barbie and Ken's adventure in New York, going to a ballet then riding to the top of the Empire State Building and saving the world from an alien invasion, but I fell asleep before he got to the end. I didn't explain to him that my dad's stories were one of my favorite parts of my childhood, and how much I wished I could hear his voice one more time. But Ethan's offer to tell me a story, so quick after my one memory, touched my heart in ways I hadn't expected.

I remembered waking up once, an hour or so later, needing water. Ethan was busy with something in my room and rushed to my side in an instant. He saw I was a little better and left the room so I could change into sweatpants, but he came back in when I was settled and rubbed my head again until I fell back asleep.

And then? I slept better than I had in a long time.

Ethan was proving to be...well, everything Stefan was not. Kind, considerate, interested in me and my background, and willing to do what I needed to be safe and comfortable. When Stefan and I were engaged, I had gotten motion sickness on the way to an event, and he told me to wait in the car until he was done "socializing." He was more irritated than compassionate.

And after the ballet...we definitely almost kissed. I swear his lip brushed mine. I touched my lips with my fingers, remembering his phantom touch. There was so much between us, beyond physical attraction. I'd always felt that magnetism toward him, and now he was slowly, slowly making his way into my heart.

Come on, Thea. It's still Ethan Flipping Taylor.

But...was he?

I wasn't thinking of him that way as much anymore.

Sure, he was still arrogant and flirtatious. He even admitted yesterday that he wasn't known for his modesty. But there was something almost childlike and innocent about him. It seemed like he missed out on the security and love that we all needed in our childhood, so now he looked for attention and admiration in some not-so-admirable ways. But maybe, just maybe, if he got that attention he craved, he'd go from "Ethan Flipping Taylor" to just "Ethan Taylor."

I studied his perfect face, taking my time, thankful that he wasn't awake to see me.

Ethan stirred, turning his face in my direction. His eyes opened slowly, confusion setting in. Then he saw me.

"I'm so sorry. I didn't mean to fall asleep here." He sat up, his tight shirt pulling on his muscles. "I was rubbing your head and passed out. I promise I didn't do it on purpose."

I put a hand on his shoulder. "It's fine. Really."

He raked a hand through his hair, then met my eyes with a mischievous grin. "You're not going to slap me this time?"

I laughed. "No. Definitely not."

"Definitely?" he repeated, not tearing his eyes from mine. "Wow. Things are improving here."

I met his gaze, drinking him in. "You could say that." Holding his gaze, I cleared my throat. "Thank you for last night. You really...I wasn't expecting all of that."

He nodded. "You're welcome. It was awful watching you in so much pain. How do you feel this morning?"

"Much better," I said.

"I may have done some reorganization while you slept," he said.

I slowly sat up, thankful that I didn't get a headache from the blood rushing out of my head. All of my clothes were folded into neat piles, my handbags stacked together in the corner, my shoes arranged in another corner. Even my makeup was organized on the counter of the vanity.

I stifled a laugh. "Not a fan of mess?"

"You call that 'mess?' That was a tornado on top of a

hurricane mixed with a train wreck. I don't know how you function."

"My mom would agree with you. But I know where everything is. Well, mostly."

He leaned on one elbow. The poor guy had slept in his dress shirt and slacks, and his hair was the messiest I'd ever seen. I kind of loved it. "That's supposed to be a mark of genius," he commented.

"More like laziness," I replied.

Ethan stretched his arms, then stood up. "I should get back to my room. I'm not supposed to be here, remember?" He winked, and it did funny things in my chest.

"No, yeah, of course," I stammered. "What do we have this morning again?"

"My parents got in last night, so we have breakfast at Gran's with everyone this morning."

Oh, yes. Breakfast with Nicholas and Rhonda Taylor. That was a cold dose of reality, another reminder of the company I was keeping. The last few days, removed from our home, it was easy to forget that Ethan and I were not remotely on the same playing field. But now we were going to be with his family, getting ready for the benefit tomorrow night.

He reached his arm out tentatively and smoothed down my hair. "You're sure you're okay now?"

I smiled up at him. "Yeah. I'm good. Thank you."

He let his hand linger for a moment, then brushed his thumb against my cheek. I fought the shivers that ran up my spine. "I'll see you in about an hour," he said. He pulled his hand away and left the room.

I buried my head in my hands. What was I doing? Now I

wasn't only *letting* him flirt, I was *hoping* he would. Ugh. I was causing one problem after another.

"NICHOLAS, can you pass the tomatoes, darling?"

I had gotten used to Rhonda Taylor's whiny voice at events, but I could roll my eyes at Ivy or Ashton as soon as she turned around. Here, where I was sitting *with* her at breakfast, I had to pretend her voice didn't grate on my nerves and drive me crazy. All the "darlings" were driving me nuts, too. It was cute when Rita said it, but Rhonda was such a phony, I couldn't handle it.

Nicholas kept his eyes on his phone and passed the plate of sliced tomatoes to Rhonda. I had heard him say two words to Ethan, give a quick hug to his mother-in-law, and then he promptly pulled out his phone and ignored the rest of us for the morning.

Rhonda took a couple of tomato slices and set down the platter, but I watched her cut them into tiny pieces and not take a single bite. Rhonda's relationship with her mother was interesting to watch. They both seemed genuinely happy to see each other, but there was some kind of disconnect. It couldn't have been related to money, seeing as Rita clearly had plenty to go around, but something about their relationship seemed strained.

Ethan was already different around them. A little more guarded than he was with Rita, a little more like Ethan Flipping Taylor again. At the same time, he still stayed close to me, keeping up our charade (although, was it a charade anymore?), and I always felt his eyes watching my every move. Before, where I found it kind of creepy, now it was endearing. And almost hot.

Oh, how the tables had turned.

"Thea, how was the ballet last night?" Gran asked.

"It was so beautiful. Thank you so much. And the costume designer was amazing. He showed me all around and answered all of my questions."

"What did you think, Ethan?" Gran asked.

"You went to the ballet?" Rhonda asked, her eyes wide.

Ethan turned to his mother. "Yes, Gran had two tickets last night. It was nice." He didn't say more, but placed his hand on mine. It didn't feel forced or fake, not anymore. Now it felt like it belonged there.

"Why wouldn't you see a ballet with Bethany? She begged you to go so many times." Rhonda tugged on Ethan's suit jacket sleeve. "You two were such a lovely couple. I don't know why you didn't bring *her* this week."

My eyes widened. Wow. She was bold. Not that I expected less from her, but I hadn't been the object of her ire before.

"Bethany is a good friend," he said through gritted teeth. "But I didn't want to bring her. I wanted to bring Thea." He turned his head to me, warmth in his eyes. "I went to the ballet because she wanted to. And I'm glad I went. It was one of the best nights I'd had in a long time."

Nicholas popped his head up, finally noting the conversation at hand. His steely eyes pierced mine, and he looked back and forth between me and Ethan, then zeroed in on our hands. His eyes narrowed.

Ethan noticed his father's mood and changed the subject. "So, Gran, is everything ready for Saturday night?"

She sighed dramatically. "These things are never ready. The pandas desperately need our help, but what can we do? We only move as quickly as the people working for us."

Did she not know that they weren't endangered anymore? I started to explain. "Aren't the pandas—"

A sharp shake of Ethan's head cut my sentence off. I turned my head to him, and his eyes warned me not to say anything.

Rita still looked at me. "Yes, dear?"

I cleared my throat. "Aren't the pandas...the sweetest animals? I've always wanted to hug one."

"Oh, yes. They're wonderful. But I hear their fur is quite bristly. I don't think they're as cuddly as they look."

"That's disappointing," I said.

"You can always cuddle with me instead," Ethan murmured for my ears only.

I jabbed him in the side. "No. Flirting."

"Really? You're going to pull that on me now?" he asked, squeezing my hand in his. I glanced down at our joined hands, then back at his face. I didn't know what to say. Did I still not want him to flirt? My heart said, *No way! Lay it on me, Ethan Taylor.*

Ethan's father cleared his throat, observing us.

What *did* he see? I wasn't sure myself. When had I switched from hating Ethan to wanting him? Holding hands last night was more than I usually did with any of my guy friends. I also didn't "almost kiss" any guy friends.

Who was I kidding? I didn't have guy friends.

Still, I couldn't put a label on what was happening between the two of us.

"Ethan," his father barked. "I'd like to speak with you today. There are some developments at work."

Ethan turned his attention to his father. "Can't I take a couple of days off from the office?"

"You don't get where I am without some sacrifices. I thought that's what you wanted, too."

Ethan's eyes turned down to his plate. I wasn't sure when I had last seen him look so ashamed.

"Seamstress girl," Rhonda called to me.

"Her name is Thea," Ethan said.

Rhonda waved her hand. "Right now, I need her to be a seamstress. I need some alterations on my dress for Saturday."

My eyes widened. "That's tomorrow."

"Yes, well, we had some problems with our usual tailor in Canyon Cove. Would you be able to do them for me?"

"I...well, I don't have a sewing machine."

"I can arrange for that," she replied. "The alterations are minor. A bit taken in on the waist, possibly the hem fixed a bit." She raised an eyebrow. "Besides, if your work is acceptable, I can recommend you to the other housewives."

Alterations were every sewist's nightmare. Whenever someone heard that I had a sewing machine, the first question was, "Can you hem my pants?" It's annoying and unsatisfying work. Creating a gown was a completely different story.

But if Rhonda put in a good word for me...

"Sure. I can do it."

"Wonderful." She clapped her hands. "You can come meet me in our room after breakfast."

I nodded and turned back to my breakfast.

"Did you have any other plans today?" Ethan asked me.

I shook my head. "Nothing really. You?"

He shook his head. He opened his mouth to say something, but decided against it and went back to his food. And right then, I realized I was going to miss spending the morning with him.

Weird.

Sixteen

ETHAN

I didn't miss Thea's stolen glances throughout breakfast. I wished I could just have breakfast with her and Gran again, just like yesterday. But when Nicholas Taylor was around, his presence demanded attention. Even if you weren't holding his.

It was the same as when I was a little boy. My father was hardly around, so all I had were my mother and a revolving door of nannies. But when my father was around, all focus was on him and what he wanted.

What he wanted was either to ignore me or berate me.

And all I wanted was his attention and approval.

I still did.

We finished eating and headed our separate directions. Thea, ever the sweetheart, gave Gran a hug and thanked her. Gran's eyes went wide, then her face burst into a radiant smile. Thea and my mom discussed plans for a dress fitting.

When it was my turn for a hug, Gran reached up to my

ear and whispered, "You picked a good one. Don't scare her off."

I pulled back and held Gran's soft, wrinkly hands in my own. Giving them a squeeze, I whispered back, "I'm trying my best. Good move with the ballet tickets."

She beamed. "I've been planning that since you told me about her."

No wonder she liked Thea. She recognized a fellow feisty spirit. "If you have anything else you can throw at me, I'm here for it."

"Oh, no, my boy." She patted my cheek. "It's all on you now." She gave me a little shove and sent me Thea's way.

My parents were already gone, and Thea stood alone waiting for me. It just felt...right.

"Hey," I said.

"Hey," she replied with a smile. If I could drink in that smile every day of my life, I would be a happy man.

Then she frowned. What did I do wrong this time?

"Are you...are you okay?" she asked.

I furrowed my brow. "What do you mean?"

"I don't know. You seem more...subdued."

I laughed. "As opposed to?"

She narrowed her eyes at me. "You know exactly what that's the opposite of."

I stared at the door my parents had just walked out of, trying to remember how I was acting. Was I that different around them? I had compartmentalized so many pieces of my life. Social Ethan. Work Ethan. Son Ethan.

Who was I really?

Taking a moment to look at Thea, *really* look at her, I

wondered at what moment she had become attuned to my personality and could sense the difference.

And then I realized I felt the most like myself when I was with her.

"Things with my dad are strained," I explained slowly. "I have to be careful around him."

She held my gaze, not shying away from me. When did that change, too? "Careful how?"

"He has expectations. Like Amy's parents."

"Amy, who's now way happier that she's cut ties with her crazy parents and married the man she loves?"

Touché. "But she never enjoyed the world of high society."

"And you do?"

I shrugged. "I enjoy having nice things, and having people think I look good and that I'm successful. Is that so bad?"

She opened her mouth, about to argue with me that my concern with appearances *were* so bad. After just a few days together, I knew the way she wanted to disagree with me. But she hesitated and closed her mouth. "I'm not sure," she finally said.

She glanced over her shoulder back at Gran, who was busy pretending that she wasn't watching us while shuffling papers. "I think that's not genuine happiness," she said. "Do you have people you love who love you back? People who know who you are without all the flashy things and still want to hang out with you? Because if the only people who want to be with you are the ones who know you for your status or the things you own, they aren't true friends."

A sudden pang filled my chest. Thea saw right through it

all. I *was* lonely. That was why I was so desperate to get her to come with me. I knew she saw through *me*, and she didn't want any of the act that I put on for everyone else. She was genuine, and she wanted me to be the same.

"For what it's worth," she continued softly, "I actually like the Ethan underneath it all better than the Ethan who's showing off for everyone."

I held her gaze another moment, waiting for her to look away. She didn't. She was my equal, unafraid of telling me how it was.

Man, I loved her.

Hold up.

Love?

That's a little crazy, right? Sure, I'd been watching her from afar for about a year, but we had really only spent a few days together.

But every moment I was with her, I felt like I could just be myself. No pretense, no showiness.

And it was incredible.

I cleared my throat, afraid she could see exactly what was going on in my mind. "The Ethan underneath it all, huh? Like, shirtless Ethan?"

She rolled her eyes and shoved me hard. "No flirting!"

I laughed, but grabbed her hand and used my other hand to grab her waist, pulling her close to me. "You can't say that you weren't flirting a second ago, too," I breathed.

Her mouth opened and closed like a fish. "That was *not* flirting!"

"Maybe it wasn't traditional flirting, but it was definitely *emotional* flirting." I winked at her.

She blinked a few times, replaying our conversation. I

heard her breath catch in her throat, the heat in her body radiating off of mine.

"Oh, you two could be in a play!" Gran called and clapped her hands. Then she whistled like she was at a baseball stadium. Apparently, she didn't care about pretending to not watch us anymore.

Thea pushed off of me, her cheeks flushed. "Sorry, Rita," she said. "I should go meet with Rhonda." She nodded at me, gave a tiny wave of her hand, and scurried out of the room.

I watched her leave, then turned back to Gran. "How was that?" I asked.

"You've got it, my boy," she replied with a wink.

I STEPPED INTO THE HALLWAY, bracing myself for a work conversation with my father. That paper company seemed like an HR disaster about to strike, but I had done my job the best I could.

"What are you doing with that girl?" he barked.

Wait, what? I quirked an eyebrow at him. "What do you mean?"

He shook his head. "She's a nobody. Why would you bother bringing her here?"

"I don't see why it matters. You've never cared about the women I brought along as dates before."

"This one is different," he hissed. "I can see the way you look at her. You actually care about this one. The others were just there to make you look good."

Apparently, he noticed more than I expected, even while he had his phone commanding his attention.

"So?" I asked. "I don't see why it matters to you."

"We have a reputation to uphold," he said. "You are *my* son. We don't need to be associated with trash like that."

I flinched. Trash? That was too far. "Mom doesn't seem to have a problem associating with her."

"Professionally. Girls like her are 'the help.' Doesn't she serve our events, too? Everyone knows her as the catering girl. How could you lower your standards like that?"

Once again, he was more perceptive than I gave him credit for. I didn't expect him to recognize Thea from any other girl. My father, who had spent years upon years ignoring me and choosing Scott in my place, suddenly interested in my romantic life? This was an infuriating turn of events.

Speaking of Scott...

"I'm surprised you're not upset about Scott's involvement with Ivy Jones, then."

"Oh, I am. But he's not my son."

"He's your *partner*," I seethed. Instead of me.

He waved his hand at me. "I can't dictate how he runs his personal life. Those are his own mistakes to make. Besides, they won't last." He pointed his finger at me. "And I'm not talking about Scott right now. I'm talking about you. No son of mine will be tangled up with the help."

If I were in an anime cartoon, there would be some intense graphics showing the anger radiating off my body. I couldn't believe this was happening. My father basically ignored me most of the time, and I spent every hour at work trying to make him happy. He was happier when I brought "floozies" to events, but now that I had someone I genuinely cared about, he wanted me to break things off?

"Don't bring her to your grandmother's event," he said, interrupting my thoughts.

"What?"

"Don't. Bring. Her. She is not welcome."

"How can you say that? This is Gran's event, not yours."

"You are part of my family. Your reputation is tied to mine." His eyes softened for a moment. He raised his hand and settled it heavy on my shoulder. "You're my son, Ethan. My legacy. I only want what's best for you. You need to make your way in this world, and I'm here to guide you. You've had fun floundering around, but now it's time to get serious about your life and your business." He pulled his hand away, clasping his hands behind his back. "If you can sacrifice for your family, then I may have plans for you at the firm. But first, prove your loyalty."

I stared at him, slack-jawed. This was the first time he had *ever* mentioned a potential promotion. My mind started spinning with the possibilities.

He held my gaze for a solid moment, longer than I could remember for the last ten years. With a single pat on my shoulder, he turned and strolled down the hall.

I stood in place, dumbstruck. For once, he actually seemed to care about my future.

And I cared about it too, right? That's why I was working so hard to make my way in our community. I had a reputation to uphold.

I turned back toward Gran's door, startled when I saw Thea standing there. Her sad eyes met mine. How long was she standing there?

"Hey," I said softly, holding my cards to my chest. I tried to gauge by her expression what exactly she had heard.

"Are you okay?" she asked.

I nodded. "You know, Nicholas Taylor just doing his best to build me up," I said with a laugh.

Her face didn't change. Maybe she heard everything he said about her. I cringed internally, waiting for the moment that she'd ask.

But instead, she rested her hand on my shoulder, the same spot where my dad had touched me a moment before. The difference between them was an ocean apart. Thea's touch was comforting, where my father's felt like the weight of the world on my shoulders.

"I'm here for you, whatever you need," she said. She let her hand run down my arm, to my hand, and laced her fingers in mine. "You're more than he thinks."

She squeezed my hand once, then walked away. I stood still, watching her, shaken by the decision I needed to make. Which would I choose—my future or the girl of my dreams?

Seventeen

THEA

Poor Ethan.

I knew he wanted to make his parents happy. Who didn't? I heard little of their conversation, but I could gather that Nicholas was pushing Ethan to be more serious about his future. In that small moment, it was like I got a peek into his childhood, and my heart broke again for him. How must he have felt, starved for love and attention, while his parents entertained others and ignored their own son?

I walked down the hotel hallway toward Rhonda's room with a little wobble in my step. Underneath the facade he presented, Ethan was genuinely fun and charismatic, but also considerate. The way he took care of me last night when I got sick was startling, but also fit the pieces that were coming together in his personality. Slowly, slowly, he was chipping away and melting the ice cube I had frozen around my heart.

Things were moving and changing with him by the

minute. The way he pulled me close and accused me of flirting with him, a half teasing but smoldering glint in his eye, sent shivers down my spine and set me on fire. I hadn't felt that kind of passion with anyone before.

And beyond all of that, he made me feel like I was truly adored. Stefan never made me feel that way. Stefan told me I was beautiful, but it was always for his own benefit. He enjoyed toting around the ballerina on his arm, saying my grace helped me fit in even though I "didn't belong" at his events. But what did Ethan do? He invited me to come with him, as his date, never mentioning how unusual my presence was. And somehow, he saw me better than anyone else ever had.

He was breaking me down, bit by bit. And as much as I thought I hated him...maybe I didn't hate him anymore. Maybe—

"Thea, darling!" Rhonda's door opened before I could even knock, startling me out of my thoughts.

"Hello, Rhonda," I said, stepping through the doorway.

She closed the heavy door behind us. "Hayk brought some sewing pins and things," she said, gesturing to a basket on the coffee table. "I'll get my dress on and come back out," Rhonda said. I nodded, and she disappeared.

I spun in a slow circle, taking in the second most elaborate hotel room I'd ever seen. The first, of course, was Gran's. But did that count when she actually lived there? So maybe this was the first most elaborate hotel room. Chandeliers, ornate couches, a piano, a pool table. Rhonda disappeared into the bedroom, and I was dying to peek at their fluffy bed.

Ew. But that's where Nicholas Taylor slept. Never mind.

Was I supposed to sit? Keep standing? Play the piano? I

wasn't sure where I belonged and awkwardly shifted back and forth on my feet, deciding what to do.

Thankfully, Rhonda emerged a moment later in a black, floor-length evening gown. One shoulder was exposed, and sequins cascaded down the front in a diagonal pattern.

"What a beautiful gown," I said. It truly was, and Rhonda looked stunning.

"Oh, thank you, dear," she said, running her hands down the front. "I'm afraid it's a little loose, though. Don't you think?"

I reached my hands out to her sides and pinched, feeling how little space there was. "It has a bit of room. But do you really want it that tight for the evening?"

"Yes, yes, of course. If you could take it in a bit, that would be wonderful."

I nodded. Honestly, I would not have changed it. Most dresses need room to move (and eat), but I wasn't one to question Rhonda Taylor's requests. I could probably take it in just enough to feel more fitted, but leave space so it didn't burst open.

Grabbing the pins from the coffee table, I knelt down in front of her and started putting them in the dress to create the new waist seams. I waited for Rhonda's whiny voice to complain about something—the lighting, the view, my sewing, the lack of fluffy pillows on the couch—but...nothing. She didn't say a word, just silently stood there while I pinched and pinned.

I glanced up at her face, expecting to see her staring at me, casting her judgment, but her eyes gazed off into the distance, her face somber and still. And...sad? She looked sad.

"Is everything all right?" I asked.

What was I thinking? Why did I need to ask Rhonda Taylor if she was all right? What in the world possessed me to open this can of worms?

She blinked a few times, as if she didn't even remember I was there, then glanced down at me. "Yes, of course. Everything is fine."

I nodded and resumed my work. Okay, then. She said everything was fine. No need to pry.

But the silence stretched out, more and more awkward.

"Did you grow up here?" I asked.

Oh, my goodness. What was wrong with me? Why did I feel compelled to get her to keep talking? It was probably my nerves. I had never seen Rhonda so subdued.

She nodded, her gaze out the window again. "Yes, I grew up here. It was just me and my mother. My father passed away when I was young."

A lump appeared in my throat. I tried to swallow it down, but it firmly stayed in place. "I'm sorry to hear that. I...um... my father passed away a few years ago."

She looked back down at me again, unusual tenderness in her eyes. "I'm sorry."

My eyes filled with tears. "Thank you." I blinked them away quickly, returning to her dress. Why was Rhonda Taylor offering *me* comfort?

"We were fine here on our own, but I tired of the city," she continued. "The beach always fascinated me, so I went out to Orange County for a summer and fell in love with Canyon Cove."

"And Nicholas?"

She laughed. "I fell in love with the *idea* of Nicholas."

My eyes widened, but I kept my gaze down.

"And now, look at me. A true trophy wife." She laughed sarcastically. "But, no matter. It's the life I always wanted." As if realizing she revealed too much to someone beneath her, she transformed her face back to the Rhonda I recognized. "Are you almost done yet?"

"Yes, almost done," I said, fumbling with the pins and pricking my finger on one. I hissed under my breath and stuck my finger in my mouth, giving her dress a last look-over. "I think you're all set. Can you take it off by yourself?"

She glanced down at the pins. "Probably not." She whirled around and breezed into her bedroom. I followed eagerly, excited to see this giant bedroom, even if it was where Nicholas Taylor slept.

It was exactly like I imagined, a giant fluffy bed with a gorgeous canopy. An incredible view of the city, which must have lit up like fireflies at night. A chandelier above the bed that made me a little nervous in case of an earthquake, and then I remembered we weren't in Southern California and New York didn't really get earthquakes.

"Wow," I breathed. "It's beautiful."

Rhonda looked around, confused. "I suppose. It's just like every other room."

Apparently, she had not stayed in the Motel 6 in San Diego. Because that was nothing like this room. But maybe after years and years of incredible lodging, you lose your excitement over luxury.

She turned her back to me, and I carefully unzipped her dress. I held back my gasp at the sight of her spine. She was skin and bones.

"I should be able to finish this up today," I stammered.

"Fabulous." She must not have noticed my reaction.

"Have the hotel send the dress to my room after you're done." With her back to me, she stepped out of her dress and walked into the giant closet.

I picked up the dress and tucked it under my arm, processing what I'd just learned and seen. Having been around food-averse ballerinas for years, I was pretty sure Rhonda had some kind of illness or an eating disorder. Ethan alluded to something the night we had pizza, but seeing it with my own eyes hit me hard.

On top of that, she openly admitted that she and Nicholas had an unhealthy relationship. And our connection over our fathers...my head was spinning.

I hurried out of her room and ran down the hall to my room, where a Bernina sewing machine waited for me. Running my fingers over it, I examined all the features of the machine that cost more than my rent for the month. Now this was something to smile about. I sat down at the table and got to work.

Eighteen

THEA

"It's perfection, Thea. Thank you so much." Rhonda was using her whiny voice again. Her words rang through the hotel room phone into my skull, and I had to yank it away for a second to gather myself.

I sent the dress back to her room around three in the afternoon, then waited with bated breath for her response. I was pretty confident in my skills, but I could never be sure what she would think. Dresses are personal, and women put so much importance on the smallest details. An hour later, I finally got her call through the hotel phone and could breathe again.

"That's great, Rhonda. I'm so glad you like it."

"Yes, I'll definitely recommend you to my friends when we get home."

"Great. Thanks again."

I hung up the phone, then fell back on my bed, arms and legs spread wide like I was making snow angels. The stress that weighed my chest down was completely lifted, and all I wanted to do was celebrate.

With Ethan.

I had been holed up in my room all day and hadn't seen him at all. And, as I expected this morning, I missed him. More than I would have ever expected a week ago.

Without thinking another moment, I embraced my desires and opened my adjoining door. Ethan's door was closed. Boldly, I knocked.

He opened a moment later, his hair rumpled and messy. He had on a white t-shirt and sweatpants, and I got a crazy urge to give him an enormous hug and snuggle up to him. *Pull it together, Thea. Keep it casual.*

"Hey," I breathed. So much for casual.

"Hey," he said, a crooked smile lighting his face.

"Were you napping?"

He nodded. "I was a little tired after last night."

Last night. Was it really last night when he took care of me and slept on the floor of my room?

"I'm so sorry," I said. "I should've called or texted first."

He shook his head, leaning against the doorway with his arms crossed over his chest. *Hello, biceps and forearms.* "It was time to wake up, anyway. Did you finish my mom's project?"

I nodded, a big grin on my face. "Yep. And she loved it." I channeled my energy and made the conscious decision to put myself out there with Ethan. "So I wanted to celebrate with you."

His eyebrows lifted, and his crooked grin turned into a full-fledged smile. "With me?" he repeated.

I kept my eyes locked on his and nodded.

A flash of indecision crossed his face. That was unexpected. For once, here I was, basically begging Ethan to go out on a date with me. And he was considering turning me down.

Heat rushed to my cheeks. Rejection from Ethan was completely unexpected. "Or, you know, I could go by myself. That's cool. If you need to do something else—"

"No, of course not. I'd love to go with you. Give me a minute to get ready." He left the door open and wandered back into the room, hiding in the bathroom. He reemerged in a dress shirt and slacks, as usual, but I couldn't decide which I preferred: dressy Ethan or napping Ethan. Ugh. I couldn't peel my eyes away from him.

"What did you have in mind?" He grabbed some hair product and ran his fingers through his hair, keeping his focus on his reflection in the vanity mirror.

I blinked a few times, repeating his question in my mind. "How about we try to get dessert again, like last night?"

He turned his head to face me. "That sounds great," he said. "I'll text Hayk to pick us up."

Ten minutes later, we emerged from the hotel lobby into the open, humid air. Grateful for the thin maxi dresses I packed, I looked over at Ethan in sympathy. "It can't be fun wearing your dress shirts and slacks in this heat."

He shrugged. "I have nothing else with me."

I widened my eyes in glee. "You know I could remedy that for you," I said.

He waved his hands at me. "I'm good."

I laughed. "Let's go."

Hayk stood by the car, holding the door open for us. "Hello, Thea," he said. "I'm glad to see you're feeling better."

I squeezed his arm. "Thank you. Ethan took good care of me last night."

"Oh?" Hayk asked, winking at Ethan.

"I mean...not anything like that!" I exclaimed. But was it like that? After our almost-kiss, there was a crazy electricity buzzing between us. And the way he told me stories and stroked my hair—it wasn't just a friendly comfort. There was something heavy and charged about last night.

Focusing on this moment, I climbed into the car. "No more looking at your phone," he said, climbing in behind me. "I want to make sure we get our dessert this time."

I laughed. "No problem. It's safely tucked away in my purse."

He nodded once, relaxing in his chair. Hayk drove us west, up Broadway, and stopped on the corner of a small residential area. He parked the car and opened the door. "Here we are. The bakery is down that street. You'll smell it before you see it."

Ethan climbed out, and I gasped out loud. "Are we going to Chunks?" I asked.

Hayk smiled. "You've heard of it?"

"Of course I have! They're Insta-famous."

"I don't know what that means, but I'm glad you're happy," Hayk said. "Enjoy your cookies."

"Thank you!" I skipped out of the car and bounced next to Ethan. "I've been hearing about these cookies for years. I can't believe I didn't already ask you to go."

Ethan reached his hand out and grabbed mine, squeezing it. "I'm glad this all worked out."

He started to pull his hand away, but I held it tighter. Why was he backing away from me? Some kind of distance was growing between us, which didn't make sense after everything we had been through together the night before.

Maybe I needed to be a little more forward.

He turned his head to look over at me, a question in his eyes. I grinned at him, trying to put him at ease, but his smile had a hint of hesitation behind it. My chest tightened a bit, concerned that maybe I had misread the signals last night. But he squeezed my hand again and held tightly as we followed our noses to the chocolate chip cookie factory.

The line was pretty long, leading into a tiny shop down a few steps from the sidewalk. Ethan stayed unusually quiet during our wait in line.

"What did you do today?" I asked, finally breaking our silence.

He turned to face me. "I tied into the office remotely and did some work."

I raised an eyebrow at him. "Really? I thought you said you didn't need to do any work while we're here."

"Yeah, that's what I thought, too," he said under his breath, turning his attention back to the line.

"Is that what your dad wanted to talk to you about?" I asked.

He hesitated a moment, eyes focused on the people ahead of us in line. What could have been so bad that he didn't want to share? "He thinks I need to make better choices. To carry the family name and take my place at the company."

"Is he offering you a better place in the company?"

"Possibly." He clenched his jaw.

Shouldn't he have been happier about this? I wanted to ask more, and it wasn't like him to be so secretive. But he looked so tense, the opposite of the Ethan I had gotten to know over the last few days.

I squeezed his hand. "I'm sorry."

He looked over at me, a softness in his gaze. "Why are you sorry?"

I shrugged. "I can tell there's something about him that gets to you. Makes you feel like you're less than you are."

"And who am I exactly?" he asked.

I peered into his eyes, wondering the same thing myself. Who was he to me now? Was he still Ethan Flipping Taylor? Or had he turned into someone else?

Was he really a different person? Or was the change in my perception of him?

Was I too quick to judge him before?

His face sobered as he waited for my response. His grip on my hand loosened, as if he were waiting for me to pull away and realize I still despised him after all. But that wasn't true, not at all.

"You're Ethan Taylor," I finally said. "Confident, cocky, but underneath, you're a big softie."

He laughed out loud again, and I couldn't help the grin that spread on my face. I was so happy to make him laugh, especially after whatever his dad said to him.

He pulled my arm and tucked me into his side, holding me tight in a sideways hug. I felt his lips press a kiss to the top of my head, and warmth filled me all the way to my toes. "Thank you," he whispered.

I turned my face up to his, furrowing my brow. "What for?"

"I know I can count on you to be honest with me. So, if

you see something good in me, then I feel like I can believe it."

He leaned his forehead down to mine, and I sucked in a breath. Our lips were just inches apart. Was he going to kiss me? Right here, right now, in the middle of the sidewalk?

But a moment later, his face changed, and he pulled his head away from mine. Disappointment filled my veins. His fingers traced the inside of my arm, down to my fingertips, but he didn't hold my hand again. I crossed my arms over my chest, wondering where I had gone wrong in this conversation.

Finally, it was our turn. We stepped into the tiny shop, a tiny space with a giant counter and a sliver of ground to stand on. The smell of freshly baked cookies nearly made me drool. Changing my focus on the cookies in front of me, I excitedly looked over the menu.

"Which cookie do you want?" he asked.

"All of them," I laughed.

"We'll take one of everything," he said to the girl behind the counter.

"No!" I exclaimed. "I was just kidding."

"It's fine," he said. "This way, you can try a bite of each cookie and decide which one is best. You need a fair judging system."

We gathered our cookies and milk and headed to an empty table with two chairs across from each other outside the tiny shop. My first pick was the classic chocolate chip with walnuts. It was the size of a giant muffin and smelled incredible. I closed my eyes and took a bite. Heaven.

"This. Is. Amazing." I opened my eyes to see Ethan

staring at me, not touching any of the cookies in front of him. "Aren't you going to try one?"

"Sure. But watching you is very entertaining," he said.

I took the cookie I had just bitten and held it up to him. He took a bite, closed his eyes, and groaned. "Okay. Best cookie ever," he relented.

"Right?" I wiggled in my seat, so excited to try the rest. I set the cookie down and tried to decide on my next test subject.

Ethan laughed. "You're adorable."

I glanced back up at him, warmth filling my chest. I knew most girls didn't like being called adorable, but I loved it.

Ethan's lips turned into a frown. "Aren't you going to tell me not to flirt?"

I looked him straight in the eyes. "No."

He swallowed hard, and I was pretty sure I got my meaning across.

The question was what he would do now.

Nineteen

ETHAN

"So, I can flirt now?" I asked with a wink.

Better to make light of the situation than draw attention to it. That was my motto with Thea.

"Within limits," she said.

"And what limits are those?"

"No asking me to take a 'ride' in your car." She even used the air quotes.

I laughed out loud. "One day, I'll *drive* you in my car, and you'll regret making such a big deal out of that one phrase."

She crossed her arms over her chest. "There's no way that's what you meant the first time we met."

"You're right," I admitted. "I was being kind of gross then." I swallowed. "Truly, I am sorry for acting that way with you."

She visibly relaxed. Did that one sentence really bother her that much? I couldn't believe it had been a full year since that night, and it still affected her.

"What changed?" she asked softly.

"A slap to the face," I said with a smirk, and she giggled. "But, in all seriousness, Amy."

"Really?"

I nodded. "Her assignment to speak her truth changed her life. She did everything just to make others happy, and it was breaking her. She's so much happier now."

"I don't see how that applies to being gross and suggestive."

I popped another bite of cookie into my mouth, trying to figure out how to explain it to her. "I have a reputation. The playboy. Every event, I have a different woman who's dying to be Ethan Taylor's date for the night."

She rolled her eyes. "You're sounding gross again."

"No, I'm not," I protested. "It's a fact."

"Fine. Continue."

"Saying things like that was part of it. Honestly, I kind of enjoyed seeing how far I could go and how much I could get away with. It was a game to me."

"And I was the first one to tell you that you were an idiot."

"First you, then Amy. Amy told me straight up what she thought of me, and she was right. And I loved it. I don't want people who are going to lie to me and pretend everything I say and do is acceptable. So once she started calling me on my faults, I started seeing myself more clearly."

Except when it came to my dad. He was the one person who could tell me I wasn't doing things right, and it stung.

But did I really want his life? Is that who I wanted to be?

As if reading my thoughts, Thea spoke. "But you question yourself around your parents."

I nodded. "What kid doesn't want to make his parents happy?" I asked with a shrug.

"It doesn't help that you're working for him, but he's promoting Scott instead of you."

I scoffed. "Don't get me started on Scott."

"What's wrong with Scott?" she asked. "For real. I see nothing wrong with him."

"He's the golden boy," I replied. "He can do no wrong. It drives me crazy. My dad puts him on a pedestal and compares me to him, but we're two completely different people."

She nodded, processing my words. "But," she said, proceeding cautiously, "is that Scott's fault?"

"Does it matter?" I asked, defensive. "All I know is that he stole my dad's attention away from me. I don't like him."

"It *does* matter," she replied. "You could look at him as an ally instead of an enemy."

"Why do you care so much?" I asked.

She blinked a few times, taken aback by my question. Maybe that was a little harsh. "Because Ivy is my friend, and I trust her judgment with Scott. And didn't Amy reconcile with him, too?" She shrugged. "I don't know. I don't want you hurting yourself with an imagined rivalry that steals your peace."

I shook my head. "It's not imagined."

"But Ivy says that Scott has nothing against you."

"I don't want to talk about Scott anymore."

"Fine." She angrily popped another piece of cookie into her mouth. She was visibly annoyed, which was the first time she was irritated with me for reasons other than "smarminess." But, to be honest, I was a little annoyed with her, too. I didn't want her to keep pushing the Scott issue. I knew how I felt about him, and that was that.

Good. Maybe she would realize that there wasn't anything that would work between us. Maybe I wouldn't have to decide between Thea and my father, after all. It would be easier this way.

But I still didn't want things to be awkward at this moment. Not until after the trip. I took in a deep breath, pushing away my feelings of frustration. "How was everything with my mom today?" I asked, trying to change the subject to neutral grounds.

"Good," she said. "She was...not what I expected."

"Really? How so?"

She chewed thoughtfully. "She told me a bit about her past. Growing up here with her mom, her dad passing away when she was young. I didn't know we had that in common."

"I hadn't thought about that either," I commented. How strange, finding a connection between my mother and Thea. I never would have thought there was anything similar between them. "How...how did your father die?"

"Cancer." She blinked away a few tears that had formed in her eyes and took another bite of her cookie.

I laid my hand on top of hers. "I'm sorry. Even from the few things you've told me about him, I know you loved him very much."

She nodded. "Thank you." She took in a deep breath and straightened. "So, your mom and I have that in common. And she told me how she ended up in Orange County." She bit her bottom lip. "I have to ask though...does she have an eating disorder?"

I sighed. "I think she might. But I haven't been comfortable enough to ask her about it."

Thea nodded. "That can be a very sensitive subject." She took another bite of cookie, taking her time. "Well, overall, she seemed like a completely different person."

I knew what she meant. "She's actually not that bad in real life. And her voice isn't normally that high-pitched."

"Right?" She laughed out loud. "I don't know how she can do it."

"You didn't know her before the show," I said.

Thea tilted her head, urging me to explain.

This conversation was getting deeper by the minute. I had no one to really share these things with, and my palms were getting clammy. Or maybe it was just the humidity.

Did I want to keep sharing with her? We were going beyond our surface territory and moving into dangerous waters.

I studied her open expression, patiently waiting for me to explain. And I realized that there was no one I really wanted to talk to more than her.

"The opportunity for the show came up about five years ago. My mom was in a really dark place." Images of my mom lying in bed all day surrounded by alcohol flashed across my vision.

"Dark, how?" Thea asked.

"She completely lost herself. My dad hardly paid any attention to her, and I had moved out and was busy living my own life. I came home one afternoon and found her passed out drunk on the couch."

Her eyes widened. "That's intense."

I nodded. "I found out about the show soon after that and sent the casting call to her."

She laughed. "So *you're* the one to blame."

I shrugged. "Depends on how you look at it. To me, it saved her life. It gave her a purpose. And she knows she's playing a role, just like me."

Her face sobered. "Then maybe you're not so bad after all."

The heavy conversation was too much for me. "I can be bad sometimes," I said, raising my eyebrows.

"Ugh, gross," she said. But this time, she smiled, knowing a joke when she heard it.

We ate our cookies for a few more minutes, making comments about which ones were our most and least favorites. We packed everything up to save for later, and I texted Hayk to pick us up while we stood on the sidewalk and waited for him.

"I have to ask one more thing about your mom," Thea said.

"Sure," I replied.

"What was your dad doing throughout all of that?" she asked.

I sucked in a breath. "Working," I replied.

"But when he was home? Didn't he notice your mom's struggle?"

Of course not, I wanted to say. But then I remembered how perceptive he was this morning at breakfast. He knew exactly what was happening between me and Thea, with just a couple glances our way.

The sad reality hit me hard. "I think he didn't care," I said.

"Wow." She ran her hand across my back, sending a shiver down my spine. Her light touch made me more unhinged than any kiss I'd had over the last few years. "Now it's my turn to say I'm sorry."

I nodded, at a loss for words, feeling the comfort and care of this incredible woman beside me.

"I wonder..." she began, then swallowed hard. "I wonder if I would have turned out like your mom. If things with Stefan hadn't ended."

"If you hadn't caught him cheating?"

She shook her head. "When I caught him, he asked me to stay with him. That whatever he was offering me as his wife would be worth enduring his 'wandering eyes.'" She shuddered. "Thankfully, my dad taught me to accept nothing lower than first place in a man's eyes. It wasn't even a question to me." She rubbed my back one more time. "I hope your mom finds some kind of peace, whatever that looks like for her."

If my father thought she would bring me down, he was dead wrong. The only thing Thea did was lift me up. Offer comfort when I had none. Share my burden and sympathize with the pain I had kept hidden away from the world for years.

Nicholas Taylor wanted a wife who would look good on his arm and improve his status. End of story. He didn't want a life partner, someone to share his joys and sorrows. My mother was a prop to him.

I wanted more than that.

I wanted Thea.

But there was more than just my happiness on the line. It

was my reputation, my place in this world. I *needed* to follow in my father's footsteps.

Call it selfish or shallow, but I enjoyed the praise and esteem I received from the people in my world. I enjoyed being known as the guy who had the most beautiful woman on his arm, with the flashy car and expensive clothes. It mattered to me.

Did I really want to lose that...for her?

I wasn't sure.

$$Twenty$$

THEA

After our cookie excursion, Ethan said he had some appointments he had to handle, so I had the evening alone. I took a little stroll down Fifth Avenue, admiring the shops, imagining my designs one day being in the windows. I could see it. I just needed my big break.

Ethan seemed kind of secretive about his plans, so I didn't pry. It was strange, after everything we had shared over the last few days. I thought we didn't have many secrets between us anymore. In some ways, he knew more about me than even Ivy did. He was my confidante, and on top of that, I couldn't deny the attraction between us.

Well, scratch that. He denied it this afternoon. If he ever had an opportunity to kiss me, it would have been today. I thought I gave him all the signals he was looking for.

I headed back to the hotel, needing some time to decompress and process what was going on. As much as I'd love to talk to Ivy, I knew she was biased. She was definitely Team

Thean, which she said was our celebrity couple name. Either that, or Ethea. She set up a poll on Instagram and said she'd update me with the results.

Clearly, I needed my mom.

"Hey, love bug," she said, picking up after the first ring. "How's New York?"

A pang filled my heart. How long had it been since I'd seen her? Two months? Three? As grateful as I was for her support of my dreams, not nagging me to come visit her, she was my mom. My comfort.

"It's been...confusing."

"Handsome, charming men often do that to us."

"You can say that again." I flopped on my bed. "How did you know?"

"Because he reminds me of your father."

"There is absolutely no way." My father's face flashed in my mind, memories of the gentle man who would tell me bedtime stories and talk late into the night about my problems. He and Ethan were complete opposites.

"You don't know what your father was like before you were born."

"Mama. You haven't even met Ethan before."

"Well," she huffed, "Google has a lot of information about Ethan Taylor."

"Oh, do they now?" I laughed. "Tell me what you found out."

"That he switches dates as often as he switches underwear. And that he's the most sought-after bachelor in Orange County."

"Doesn't that sound like someone else we know?" I asked, refusing to say Stefan's name.

"Similar, but there are some glaring differences. I found a picture from last summer of Ethan walking around Central Park with his grandmother. It looked like they were feeding pigeons."

An unbidden smile filled my face. Our meetup in the park seemed like ages ago, when I tried to run away from Ethan and he washed the bird poop out of my hair. The way he treated his grandmother was enough to remind me he wasn't the same as Stefan.

And beyond that, he truly cared about his mother. When his dad didn't care enough about her well-being, Ethan saved her. In a weird way, to be sure, but it still was an act of kindness for someone other than himself.

"I don't know, Thea," she continued. "He may have this appearance to everyone else, but I think someone who loves his grandmother like that must be a good person."

I sighed. "I think you're right."

"So you like him now?"

"More than like him. *Like* like him."

"Are you in sixth grade again? Is this like Dylan Rossini?"

"More than Dylan Rossini."

Mom blew out a breath. "That's serious."

"You're telling me."

"What changed?"

I chewed my bottom lip, trying to pinpoint the exact moment when I started feeling differently about him. There were so many moments that all added up, finally giving me an accurate picture of who he was.

"I think I didn't know who he really was," I admitted.

"And now?"

Good question, Mama. Who was he? Moments of this

week flashed in rapid succession. His thumb brushing my lip in Hayk's car. His hands on my waist when I slipped in the rain. Holding his hand at the ballet.

His explanation of his childhood in the airport lounge. Our conversation in the pizza shop, and again today at Chunks about his mother and how he wanted to keep her healthy and safe. The way he took care of me when I got sick, rubbing my head and telling me stories.

"He's a really good person," I said. "He's kind, considerate, and he cares about others. But he has a reputation that he feels like he needs to uphold. It holds him back from being who he really is in front of other people."

"Mm-hm," my mom hummed. "Just like your dad."

"Elaborate."

"When I first met your dad, he was a serial dater. Everyone knew he didn't date the same girl twice."

I laughed out loud. "Sounds familiar. And what changed?"

"He met the *right* girl."

"Wow, Mama. Cocky much?"

"It's the truth," she said, sounding so much like Ethan. Maybe there was more of him in my family than I thought.

All I knew of my father was this incredible, caring, loving man who adored my mom and his family.

Did Ethan have that in him, too?

"I don't know what to think," I said.

"Don't think so hard. You're pushing love away. You need to let love in."

Maybe she was right.

We ended the phone call, and I decided to take a walk

and call Ivy. After all, she was the one rooting for me and Ethan in the first place.

Her phone went straight to voicemail, though. I left her a quick message. "Hey girl! Thought I'd take a moment to say hi and catch up with you, but you're probably teaching privates right now. I hope everyone's doing well at the studio. Things here in New York are...a lot better than I expected. You were right about Ethan. He's not as bad as I thought. Anyway, call me back whenever you get a chance so I can fill you in on everything. I'm even taking a ballet class tomorrow. Have a good night! Talk to you soon."

I hung up my phone and meandered down the streets of the city. I loved the bright lights and busy streets. Living here would be a little too much for me, especially when people intentionally bumped into you and shoved you off the sidewalk, but there was so much energy and life that I loved to experience now and then.

I ate some street food from a vendor, praying I wouldn't get food poisoning, and headed back to my hotel for an early night in. I spent the night stretching and preparing for my class in the morning, since I was so out of shape and would otherwise be embarrassed if I wasn't ready for my first ballet class in years.

I WAS PULLING my new purple leotard on over my tights the next morning when my phone started buzzing. I flipped it over to see Ivy's name on the screen.

"Hey, Ivy! How's it going?" I asked.

"Hey, girl," she said softly. "I'm good. Things at the studio are good." She paused. "How are you?"

"Great! About to go take a ballet class at the Humphrey School."

"Cool, cool," she said.

"What's up?" I asked.

"I'm guessing you haven't been online much this morning?"

Online? I didn't spend my earliest waking hours scouring social media like Ivy, so I guessed that was unusual for her. "No, not really. Why?"

"I'm going to send you a picture." She was silent for a moment.

I put the call on speakerphone and waited for her text to come through.

It was a picture of Ethan.

Of Ethan and Carmen Valencia. The gorgeous, young fashion designer.

At dinner.

With him brushing a piece of hair away from her face, and her smiling adoringly at him.

"Oh," I said. There wasn't another word that existed in the English language. At least, not for me.

"I didn't...I wasn't sure if you would care or not. But after your voicemail yesterday, I thought maybe things had changed between you two."

She was right. Things were changing. I was definitely feeling things for him.

And now?

I was feeling different things.

"Thank you for sending this to me," I said. "I, um...I need to go."

"Thea, wait!" I heard her say as I hung up the phone.

Stupid. How could I be so stupid? I knew exactly who he was this whole time. A player. A self-centered, arrogant player. He never cared about me. I wasn't any different from the other girls he toted around. I was just another conquest for him.

Hot, angry tears filled my eyes. I couldn't believe I had fallen for his tricks. He was another Stefan. What was I thinking? I swiped the tears away from my eyes, changing the focus from my stupidity to anger with Ethan. How dare he lead me on like this? He made me feel like I was different. Like there was something special between us. Was this his game all along? Did he tell every girl the same stories about his childhood, *then* convince them to take a "ride" in his car?

I felt sick. I fell for his charm and made an idiot out of myself.

I stared at the picture of Ethan and Carmen, trying to reconcile the image in my mind with the Ethan I had been with all week. My finger slipped and scrolled back one image, the last image Ivy had sent me. The one of Ethan holding me at the airport.

I was about to swipe away in disgust, but something caught my attention. The look in Ethan's eyes. The one that had captured me the first time I saw it. He was filled with pure adoration, like I was the most valuable treasure he'd ever had the privilege of holding in his arms. I switched back to the picture of him with Carmen, and he had a smile on his lips, but his eyes weren't the same.

Maybe this picture didn't tell the entire story.

Maybe there was more to explain.

Maybe Ethan was the one who needed to tell me the truth.

Twenty-One

ETHAN

Ethan Taylor and Carmen Valencia—Hot New Couple Alert!

Spotted in NYC: Ethan Taylor and Carmen Valencia

Tender moment caught on camera between Ethan Taylor and Carmen Valencia

The notifications kept buzzing one after another. Of course, I had an alert set for my name, so any time an article was written about me, I'd see. And now, every gossip site was blowing up, exposing my supposed love connection with Carmen Valencia.

What everyone didn't know was that there were no sparks flying between the two of us. It was purely a business dinner.

I still hadn't decided what I was going to do about Thea, but a deal was a deal. I promised her a VIP experience at Fashion Week, and I had already asked Carmen to make that happen. So last night's dinner was our final meeting to nail down the specifics about the event and go through the plan for the day.

Did the cameras happen to catch the moment a fly was in her hair and I reached over to flick it away? Of course they did. That didn't surprise me.

I knew what it looked like, though.

And at this point, I wasn't sure it was such a terrible thing.

All night, I tossed and turned, wondering what to do about Thea. Was this one woman worth throwing away my reputation and my position? She was special. Absolutely. And I was pretty sure I was in love with her. But...was that enough?

The picture came out in the morning, and it seemed like the perfect way to break things off with her. She'd see it, realize that I was exactly who she thought I was, and pull away. I could still give her the experience I had promised, but we could keep a distance from each other for another day or two. I'd go home, nurse a bit of a broken heart, but I'd be back in action soon enough.

Right?

Thump, thump, thump.

"Ethan! I need to talk to you!" Thea's voice called through the adjoining door.

Here we go.

I opened the door, revealing Thea in full ballet getup. Her red hair was pulled back in a low bun, and she wore a purple leotard and tights with loose shorts over the top. Even though she claimed she had the wrong body type for ballet, I'd watch any show she performed in.

I swallowed hard. "Hey, Thea. What's up?" Better to act casual than preempt whatever conversation was coming my way.

"I saw the picture of you and Carmen."

I nodded.

"But I know you're not interested in her."

My eyes widened. "How...what makes you think that?"

She took a slow step toward me. "Because," she said, stepping closer until our bodies were nearly touching, "you weren't looking at her like you're looking at me now."

I could barely catch my breath. *No kidding. How could I look at her like that when you exist in this world?* "How am I looking at you?" I breathed.

"Like I'm the most precious thing to you." She took in a shaky breath, placing her hands on my chest and pressing her body against mine. "Like you adore me. Like you can't think about anything other than doing this."

And then she kissed me.

She kissed *me*.

Slow, but purposeful. Gentle, but confident.

I couldn't help but melt into her. Time slowed, then stopped completely. There was nothing and no one in this moment except me and Thea. All thoughts flew from my mind as I focused in on this incredible, perfect woman kissing me.

I let go of the heavy hotel door and grabbed Thea by the waist, pulling her into the room with me. Keeping my lips on hers, I leaned my back against the wall and pulled her close.

I lifted my hand and cupped her cheek, knowing exactly how precious and delicate this moment was. As I let my fingers drift down her neck, she made a small whimper in appreciation. She was like a precious bird, and I wanted to touch and feel her.

Everything I thought I knew about love paled in this moment. This was beyond any kiss in my lifetime.

I thought I loved her before.

But now?

I *knew*.

Her kisses slowed, a smile spreading on her face. I pulled away and gazed down at this incredible girl. I couldn't believe we were finally here. She finally trusted me to let me hold her. To let me kiss her.

"And that," she said breathlessly, "is how I know there's nothing going on between you and Carmen."

It was like someone dumped a bucket of cold water on my head. Carmen. My father.

What was I doing kissing Thea?

This was too much. I was supposed to be pushing her away, not bringing her into my room and kissing her senseless. I lost my head for a moment, distracted by her absolute acceptance of my feelings for her.

Focus, Ethan.

Her eyes darted back and forth, trying to process my sudden shift of emotions. "Am I wrong?" she asked softly.

I shook my head. I had told her never to lie to me, and I wouldn't lie to her either. "You're not wrong. There's nothing between me and Carmen."

A tentative smile appeared on her lips. "Then there's nothing to worry about," she said, leaning in for another kiss.

I turned my head, blocking her kiss. She reared back,

taking steps away from me. Her eyes were wide with shock and humiliation.

"There isn't anyone else," I explained. "But I'm not sure there's a real future between us."

"A future?" she repeated. "Since when has that been a concern for you? Did you ever date because you saw a future with those other girls?"

"No. But it's different with you."

"Different, how?"

Different because I'm in love with you. "I need to focus on my future. On having a woman by my side who will take me to new places and help me succeed."

Her cheeks were already pink, but now they blazed red with anger. "You're telling me I'm not good enough for you?"

"I'm not...it's not—"

"Is *this* what your dad was talking to you about yesterday? That I'm not good enough for you, and you need to ditch me? So you can find a trophy wife like your mom?"

"Not in those words exactly, but—"

She scoffed and threw her hands in the air. "You've *got* to be kidding me."

"I'm still trying to figure everything out, Thea," I said. "You don't understand what it's like to have a father like mine. He analyzes every move I make, and it's never enough. Not when Scott is there, always one step ahead of me."

"Scott, who's getting married to Ivy Jones," she said skeptically. It was the same point I had made to my father yesterday.

I was desperate to explain, to make her somehow understand. "But he's not my father's son. And he does everything in business perfectly. My dad has expectations for our family and our legacy. And part of that means that I have to be a Taylor. That means there are standards I have to adhere to for my family and the partner I choose for my life."

Her eyes nearly bugged out of her head. "That's enough," she said. "I can't believe this. I am so, so stupid." She took two steps to the door before I grabbed her arm and pulled her back to me, closing my arms around her waist one more time.

"Let me go!" she exclaimed, beating a fist against my chest.

"Thea," I whispered, and she stilled. "You're not stupid. You're incredible. Smart, beautiful, feisty, considerate...You're everything I could ever dream of." I trailed the back of my hand down her flushed cheek. "You're perfect."

She closed her eyes at my touch and melted into me.

"I wish things could be different," I whispered.

Her eyes flashed open, a fury rivaling the one she exhibited a year ago. I nearly covered my face to prepare for another slap.

"Then let me make one thing clear," she said in a low voice, sending a chill down my spine. "I *never* want to speak to you again." She shoved my chest hard and walked to the front door. She flung it open and stepped into the hallway, looking once more over her shoulder. "I had you pegged one year ago. I should have known better." She slammed the door behind her, and then she was gone.

All I wanted to do was call her name and tell her she was wrong. That there was more to me than there had been a year ago. That I was a different person, and it was all because of her.

That I was in love with her.

That she was everything I ever wanted, and now I knew I could never have.

I slid down the wall and sat on the floor, my head in my hands. I had made a mess of everything.

Twenty~Two

THEA

Stupid, stupid, stupid.

How many times in one day can a person feel like an idiot?

I can tell you, it's at least two.

Once, when Ivy sent me the picture of Ethan and Carmen. And now, when I threw myself at him—literally *threw* myself—and he rejected me.

Ethan.

Flipping.

Taylor.

After crying my eyes out in my room, washing my face with ice cold water to reduce the swelling, and gathering my ballet shoes and necessities, I headed to the subway station.

Before descending the steps of the station, I called Rita and left a quick message, telling her I would leave this afternoon. I slipped my phone into my pocket, and it was like muscle memory kicked in. Dodging and diving through the people felt like a dance I'd performed thousands of times. Finally, I sat on the subway train with my earbuds in, refusing to look at or acknowledge anyone else nearby. I needed to wallow in my idiocy.

All I needed was a ballet class. Ballet would help. Taking a class, pushing my body to its limits, pretending I hadn't just kissed Ethan.

Felt his hands on my waist.

And on my cheek.

And down my neck.

I suppressed a shiver.

How would I ever forget what it felt like to be in his arms? To have his lips on mine, the intensity in his eyes as he told me I was perfect for him? But then for him to tell me we had no future.

What was this week, then? All the shared experiences. All the revelations about his past, opening up his boyish charm and showing me the true Ethan that hid underneath the facade he showed to everyone else. Was that all...nothing? Because it wasn't *nothing* to me.

It was everything. Everything that was lacking in my relationship with Stefan. Everything that was lacking in my life.

This rejection was even more bitter than what happened with Stefan. When I found out that Stefan was cheating on me with Tabitha, it was hot embarrassment, a blow to my ego and reputation. But it didn't feel like someone had ripped my heart out and stomped on it. We had a connection, sure, but it wasn't love.

Was this...was this *love*?

Maybe I thought it was. But after the way he treated me,

there's no way that Ethan and I had anything resembling love.

The tears threatened to fall. Even though I was surrounded by strangers, some of whom were doing things much odder than just listening to music and sobbing, I refused to cry. I got off the subway at my stop. As soon as I climbed up the stairs onto the street, my phone got service again. I saw three missed calls from Ivy, two from my mom, and five text messages from Ethan. And a missed call from Rita. The others I could ignore, but after Rita's kindness this week, especially with the ballet, I felt a responsibility to explain to her. With a sigh, I dialed her number and walked toward the dance studio.

"Thea, darling!" her thin voice sang through my ear.

"Hello, Rita," I said.

"Now, what is this nonsense about you leaving early?"

I really didn't want to lie to her. I couldn't tell her we broke up, which would be the easiest explanation for her, but I couldn't call it a true "breakup" when we were never actually together. "There's been a change in my relationship with Ethan."

"Oh, my dear. Couples fight all the time."

"No, it was more serious than a minor squabble."

"Trust me. What you two have can survive this rough patch."

I put my hand to my forehead, bracing myself for what I was about to say. "Thank you, but you don't understand. Ethan and I are not really dating. We never were. We were only pretending to date to make you happy."

Silence.

Then a high-pitched, warbly laugh. "Oh, my dear. Fake dating was *my* idea."

Hold the phone. "Wait. What?"

She laughed again. "Ethan told me how much he liked you, but he didn't think you would come with him. So I told him to make up this scenario, where he needed you to pretend to be his girlfriend. Did he say his inheritance depended on it?"

"Uh, no, actually. He said that would be ridiculous."

"Ah, that's disappointing. I thought that would work."

What was with this family? One nutcase after another.

"Did it work, though?" she asked. "Did you fall for him?"

"I...I thought there was something between us." I blinked away the tears that had been hiding behind my eyes. "Look, Rita. I appreciate your concern for your grandson's love life. But when I tell you we had a falling out this morning, you have to believe me. He said he didn't think there was a place for me in his future."

She paused. "That boy..." she muttered, almost like a growl.

"So I think you can understand why I want to go home. I can't be around him again. Not after all of that."

"Thea," she said softly, almost like a whisper. "Whatever has happened with Ethan, I would like to think that you and I had a connection this week. And I know there was something special between you and Rhonda as well. Please. I would still like you to come tonight, as *my* guest."

My heart warmed, appreciative of her sentiments. "Thank you so much. I really appreciate the offer. But I can't."

"Your sewing business," she pressed. "Think of the connections you'll make."

"I am really so grateful, but—"

"The pandas, Thea!" she cut in. "Think of the pandas. They need you. Please, just come for the pandas."

"Oh, Rita," I said. How could I argue with her?

"There. It's settled. You'll come tonight. Not for Ethan, and not even for me, but for the pandas. I look forward to seeing your dress. Have a lovely afternoon." And she hung up.

I stared at my phone, wondering how that had just happened. The choice was still mine; at the end of the day, there was no obligation to come tonight. But a big part of me couldn't help feeling like I wanted to be there for Rita. Plus, this panda benefit had to be a sight to see.

And, beyond that, there was still the possibility of making connections for my sewing business. Rhonda promised to tell everyone about me, and wouldn't it be better if I was actually there, wearing my own design?

The pros and cons rattled through my brain as I let my muscle memory take over and lead me to the studio. Not much had changed in the last ten years on the Avenue of the Americas. There were still a few of the same lunch spots where I would eat with my fellow ballerinas between classes. The paint was peeling on more buildings, and the sidewalks had more cracks, but it still felt like home. I entered the Humphrey Ballet School, a tiny door that you would miss if you didn't know it was there. As I walked up the sweltering stairs, memories flashed before my eyes of playing cards with friends before pointe class, talking about the boys we partnered with and which ones wore tights that were a little too transparent.

I made my way up the four flights of stairs and to the front desk, where I paid for an open adult ballet class. There were a few extra minutes before class started, and the studio was empty. I set my bags inside, found a spot at the barre, and started stretching. This was the same room I spent hours training in all those summers ago. It had two strange white columns in the middle of the room, which was extremely inconvenient for combinations traveling across the floor, but the nostalgia hit me hard. Memories of my dad watching me in the hallway punched me in the gut, and after this morning, it was almost too much to handle.

"Breathe," I said out loud to myself.

"Thea?" Nicole Jameson's voice called to me from the doorway.

I blinked away the tears that threatened to fall. This was the first time I was going to see my favorite ballet teacher and mentor in ten years, and I wasn't about to be a blubbering mess.

"Nicole!" I called, jumping up and skipping across the floor to her. I embraced her in a tight hug, the familiar smell of vanilla coming off of her dark brown skin. Her hair had more gray in it than I remembered, but I guessed I had gotten older, too.

"I had no idea you'd be here!" she said. She pulled back and held me by the shoulders. "My, you've gotten so beautiful. Are you just visiting the city?"

"Yes, I'm here with...someone," I said, not wanting to discuss Ethan. "I'll be leaving soon, though."

"Well, I'm glad you came to take a class. I think about you often. Are you still dancing?" she asked.

"I actually teach ballet," I said, smiling as I thought about my students. "They're mostly competitive jazz students, but I love teaching them the importance of ballet in their training. And I sew most of their costumes."

"That's my girl," she said. She glanced at the clock. "We have a few more minutes before class starts. Do you have any pictures?"

I grabbed my phone from my purse and opened my photos, pulling up the album of my sewing projects. "These are some of the dance costumes I've designed recently," I said, showing her the circus themed costumes for the dance Ivy choreographed last season. I swiped through the pictures, showing her some solo costumes and ending with the pageant dress I designed for Cordelia.

"These are incredible, Thea," Nicole said, zooming in on one of the pictures. "I knew you'd find your place."

"You were right," I said. "I couldn't imagine it any other way. And I truly love what I do."

She looked back up at me and handed my phone to me. Another student walked into the room, and she waved in greeting. "I'm really proud of you," she said. "You've turned into a beautiful, strong young woman."

The tears I'd been holding all morning were back again. I blinked them away. This was not the time to give in. "Thank you. I've missed you, Nicole."

"I've missed you, too." She gave me another hug. "You look like you need a friend, though."

I looked back down at my phone. "I have a couple. But... I'm in a hard spot right now."

She squeezed my shoulder. "Let's talk after class. For now, focus on ballet."

That I could do.

"WHAT DID YOU THINK?" Nicole asked after class.

I used the towel I brought from the hotel to wipe the sweat that was dripping down my face and chest. "*Teaching* ballet is nothing like *taking* ballet," I said.

"You did a beautiful job," she said.

I laughed out loud. "I've lost so much of my technique. My turnout was awful."

"You're too hard on yourself. Did you enjoy it?"

I chewed my bottom lip. It was exactly the same thing my mom would have asked. Everything was always work to me, but was I happy? "Yes. I actually really enjoyed it."

Her face broke into a grin. "Perfect. Now come talk to me." She pulled two black teacher chairs up to the mirror, and we sat side by side.

I didn't know what it was about Nicole, but I could always talk to her and let everything out. She was the one who encouraged me to find my place after the changes in my body made a professional career in ballet an impossibility.

So I sat next to her and unloaded everything. My broken engagement with Stefan, my initial encounters with Ethan, how I realized everything had changed this week, and the disasters of epic proportions that happened this morning.

"I don't know what to do now," I said. "I don't want to face any of them after that."

Nicole hummed and sat back in her chair. "You know what I think?" she said.

"What?"

"I think that's the cowardly thing to do."

I laughed humorlessly. "Oh, really? I think Ethan and his father made it pretty clear that I wasn't welcome here."

"Who invited you?"

"Ethan."

"But I thought his grandmother told you to come."

"Yeah, I guess."

"And wasn't Ethan going to get you into Fashion Week? You deserve that, even more so after everything he put you through. Your career could take off after you make the connections this weekend."

"I don't think it's worth it anymore. I don't want to be anywhere that people don't want me."

Nicole sighed and put a gentle hand on my leg. "You know, I had many people fighting against me when I wanted to become a professional ballerina. People who said that audiences would never come to see a Black Odette in Swan Lake." She put her hand under my chin and lifted my face to hers. "They told me I didn't belong, and that I needed to leave."

"And what did you do?" I asked quietly, even though I already knew the answer.

Her face brightened in a big grin. "I told them to move out of the way, because I was making my own path, no matter what." She squeezed my cheeks once. "Make your own path, Thea. Don't let anyone hold you back from what you want or deserve."

Twenty-Three

ETHAN

I sat in the same spot on the floor, staring at my phone, willing Thea to respond. I had messaged her twenty minutes after she left, wishing I could explain more, then immediately regretting my decision to open the conversation again. She deserved so much more than I could give her. But I still wanted her.

Nothing. She ignored every one of the five messages I sent. So I stayed in my spot on the floor, kicking myself for every decision I'd made this week, because the ache in my chest would never disappear.

I was still sitting in my same spot on the floor when my phone buzzed with a call from Gran. "Hey, Gran," I said.

"Come to my apartment this instant." And she hung up.

With a sigh, I heaved myself up from the floor. My back ached from sitting in that position. Sometimes I forgot I wasn't seventeen anymore. Taking the short trek up to

Gran's apartment and saluting Roger on the way in, I found a sight I hadn't seen in many years: Gran and my mom, sitting together around the coffee table and drinking tea.

"Hey," I said slowly, sinking into the chair between them that was left for me. "I wasn't expecting you both to be here."

"Yes, well," Gran said, "your father was busy, and your mother asked to have some time with me."

My mom smiled as she met my eyes. "I had a lovely time with Thea yesterday, and she made me think about my relationship with my mother. I decided it was time to catch up."

I blinked a few times, not understanding this sudden change in heart, and turned my head to my smiling Gran. "Well, that's great," I said with a twinge of sarcasm. "Thea fixes our family relationships while I ruin everything with her."

"Yes, about that," Gran said, and then she whacked me on the shoulder.

"Hey! What was that for?"

"You stupid boy," she said. "What on earth did you do to push her away?"

I slumped back in my chair, not ready to have this conversation with anyone. "I don't want to talk about it."

"That's too bad," my mom said.

I looked back and forth between the two of them. "Since when are you two on the same team?"

They shared a glance. "We were a good team, the two of us, for a long time," Gran said softly.

"Right. Before Mom moved out to California," I said.

Gran tilted her head back and forth. "It wasn't just the distance. It was your father."

I raised my eyebrows. "You hate Dad that much?" I asked

her. "I knew there were always issues between the two of you, but I didn't know it went that far."

Gran looked over at my mom.

Mom sighed. "Your father was jealous of my relationship with my mother. He made me choose between the two of them." She huffed a laugh. "Not that he ever chose me over anyone else."

I spoke slowly, trying to make sense of her words. "So you chose to be with Dad instead of maintaining your relationship with your mother?"

She shrugged. "It seemed like it was worth it at the time. He made it seem like he had so much to offer me. That I would be his prized possession, and if I dedicated myself to him and his wants, he could make every opportunity present itself to me." She looked down at her hands, finding her words. "I wish I'd never believed him."

The words sounded eerily similar to something Thea had said just the day before. Wondering how her life would have been if she had married Stefan.

Gran placed a soft, wrinkly hand on top of Mom's. "At least he gave you a wonderful son," she said. "Speaking of whom…" And she smacked me on the back of the head.

"Jeez, Gran. Stop assaulting me."

"Where is Thea? She's the best thing that's ever happened to you."

After my mom's revelation, I wasn't so sure I wanted to share. "I told her I wasn't sure we had a future," I mumbled.

"And what gave you that idea?" Gran exclaimed. "I've never seen you so smitten. And no one calls you on your baloney like she does."

"I know, I know!" I ran a hand through my hair and stood

up, pacing to release my nervous energy. "I've never felt this way about anyone. She sees me, the *real* me, that no one really knows." I turned back to them. "Except for probably you, Gran."

"Then why on God's green earth would you ever throw that away?"

"Yesterday after breakfast, Dad said I needed to think about my future." As an afterthought, I mumbled, "And he offered me a promotion."

Gran's face twisted into disgust. "There is a special torment waiting for that man."

"Mother!" Mom exclaimed.

"Rhonda, I swear on all things holy, that man does not deserve either of you. To think that he made you choose between me and him, when he has been nothing but disloyal to you."

My mom's gaze fell toward her lap.

"Mom? Is that true?" I asked, sitting down next to her.

She looked at me out of the corner of her eyes. "Do you really think your father has been faithful to me for all these years? He wouldn't care if I died. I was the piece he needed on his arm, the old money connection he needed to make his way in this world."

I was still with shock. Sure, my mother had never said a kind word about my father, but she never disparaged him either. I never thought my parents were happy, or that they had anything resembling a functional marriage, but infidelity took it to another level. How had I been so naïve?

"How do you stand for it?" I asked. "Why do you stay?"

She smiled sadly at me. "The same reason you pushed Thea away."

I furrowed my brow, confused.

"Your father has a lot to offer," she explained. "Status, fame, living in an incredible house by the beach. I figured it was an even trade." She leaned over to me and put her hand on my arm. "But I was wrong. If it wasn't for you, I would probably be dead right now." Her eyes glistened with tears. "You deserve so much more than this life. You have to untangle yourself from your father. Otherwise, you'll end up like me."

I swallowed hard. I never thought I wanted anything other than this life. The parties, the nice car, the clothes, everything I had, I owed to my father and this lifestyle. But to have my mother tell me she was dying inside...Is that what I wanted for my future? To be my father? To have a wife I didn't care about, other than the connections she would bring me?

My head was spinning.

"Ethan, it's not too late for you," Gran said, breaking through my tornado of thoughts. "You're not so far gone."

"Are you going to stay with him?" I asked my mom, ignoring Gran for a moment. I needed that answer.

Mom looked over at Gran, sharing a meaningful, somber look. "I may stay here."

I nodded slowly, processing that possibility. Disappointment that she wouldn't be coming home, relief that she wouldn't be with my father anymore, pride that she was finally standing up for herself where she deserved.

"Then I think you're right," I said to Gran. "It's time to make some of my own choices."

She squealed. "Oh, wonderful!" she said, clapping her hands.

"But Thea said she's leaving this afternoon," I said. "I think I need to go to the airport."

"Nonsense," Gran said, gesturing to her vintage phone. "I've already talked to her."

My eyes bugged out of my head. "You have? When?"

"She left me a lovely voice message apologizing for leaving this afternoon. I called her and talked to her. I told her that the fake dating was my idea," she laughed behind her hand, "and that she was my guest, not yours."

"Did it work?"

"I wasn't sure, so I told her the pandas needed her. After that, I believe I had her convinced."

I shook my head. Hopefully Gran would never find out that the pandas weren't in as much danger as before, because she'd lose a sizeable piece of her ammunition.

"And that," she said to me, taking a sip of her tea, "is how it's done."

I stood in the center of the ballroom at 6:55 that evening, my eyes darting around the room as I watched for Thea.

Be patient, I told myself. *Perfection takes time.*

Even repeating our inside joke did little to calm my nerves. A sea of black and white surrounded me, as every attendee meticulously followed Gran's dress code. I wore a classic black tux with a black bow tie, but my shoes were a little more outgoing: black and white wingtip oxfords.

I kept scanning the room, looking for Thea and her red hair. The same reason she stood out to me over a year ago.

"She'll come," Gran reassured me, patting my arm. She had on a white suit jacket with her black dress, a white hat covering the top of her head.

I nodded in agreement but said nothing, afraid that I would betray exactly how nervous I was. I had pushed her away, and she was only coming here as Gran's guest. How would I convince her I had changed my mind? Or really, that this morning had been the exact opposite of everything I had wanted for the last year?

There she was.

Perfection truly does take time.

She was stunning. Her red hair had been softly curled, pulled over to one side. Her satin dress had a white bodice, with off-the-shoulder black cap sleeves. The skirt of the dress was full and black, but along the bottom edge were little green shoots of bamboo.

She had created an elegant panda dress.

Gran clapped her hands in delight. "Look at that dress! She really is talented."

I started walking toward her, but Gran pulled my arm. "Give her a minute. You don't want to scare her away."

Fighting against the magnetism pulling me toward her was difficult, but Gran was right. If I alarmed her too quickly, she might bolt.

She smiled at the people nearby, and the surrounding women had two reactions: either they came up to her and admired her dress, or they watched her in jealousy out of the sides of their eyes. I wasn't surprised. Thea had a presence that no one could deny.

"I'll go say hello to her first," Gran said.

She started walking toward her, and I stayed in my place to watch from a distance. But before Gran could get to her, someone else cut her off.

My father.

Twenty-Four

THEA

I gazed around the ballroom, taking in the sights in front of me. Rita spared no expense for her beloved pandas. I hoped she'd like my dress. Although I had sewn the dress itself last week, I spent the afternoon adding the bamboo accents on the skirt.

Knowing that Ethan would be here was humiliating, but talking to Nicole gave me the extra burst of confidence I needed. After everything he had put me through, I deserved to be here and make connections, even if only for my business. I was going to walk in with my head held high, as Rita's guest, and enjoy my evening.

Besides, the pandas needed me.

The glittering ballroom was covered in black and white decorations. White roses as centerpieces, black tablecloths, white chairs, but between everything were hints of green. Curious if there were any cameras, I looked for a crew, but I saw none. Apparently Rita really meant it when she said there would be no mention of the Trophy Wives show here.

I wondered if Ethan was going to bring a date with him. I wouldn't be surprised. Considering that his father expected him to maintain a certain image, I figured he would have already moved on from me. We shared one kiss and held hands a couple of times. Big deal. He had girls lined up around the block for him, as he had told me himself a few days ago.

My stomach felt sick.

A few of the other guests stopped me to compliment my dress. Few women wore skirts with this much volume, but I figured if I was going to cosplay as a panda, I had to embrace the size. At least I kept the waist small, so you could see my figure. I wished I had brought a business card, or some way to keep in touch with these contacts. Once again, Rita was right. Being here *was* good for my business.

I took a few more steps toward the center of the ball-room, but stopped short when Nicholas Taylor barreled in front of me.

"What are you doing here?" he asked in a low, dangerous voice.

I reared back in shock. Those were the first words he had ever directly spoken to me, other than to demand another drink when I was working catering events.

"I was invited," I said slowly, applauding myself for a calm and even voice, even though my heart was racing.

"The invitation has been rescinded," he replied.

My heart thumped even faster. Was he serious? This wasn't his event, right? Did he even have the right to say that?

He was Nicholas Taylor. He had the right to say whatever he wanted.

But that didn't mean I had to agree.

"You must be mistaken," I said coolly. "Rita called me personally this afternoon to make sure I came."

"That old woman doesn't know what she's talking about. I told Ethan to stay far away from you. You're ruining him. It's time for you to go." He grabbed my arm and started pulling me toward the door.

"Don't touch her." Ethan's deep voice rumbled over my shoulder. I turned to look at him, and my breath caught in my throat. As much as I wanted to be angry with him, my heart ached. I'd never denied my attraction to him; he always reminded me of a Ken doll. And now, he was Prince Ken dressed up for a ball with Princess Barbie. How I wanted to be that Barbie on his arm.

The fury in his eyes was startling, though. Especially considering that he directed his anger at his father.

"I'm just taking out the trash," Nicholas said with a sarcastic laugh.

My mouth dropped open. Wrenching my arm free from his grasp, I pointed my finger at him. "I am *not* trash!" I exclaimed. "How dare you treat people this way! You are a monster."

Nicholas got right up in my face. "Now you listen here—"

Ethan pulled me behind him and stood toe-to-toe with his father. "You will not speak to her like that," he said in a low voice. "Thea is my guest, and Gran's. You can do whatever you want back home, but she is welcome here."

"She's not welcome anywhere around me!" Nicholas boomed.

"Then you can leave," Rita said, appearing at my side. "In fact, I insist you leave. I do not want to see you again."

His jaw pulsed. "If *this* is the company you choose to keep," Nicholas said to Rita, pointing at me, "then I want nothing to do with you." He stepped right up to Ethan. "And especially not you."

"Fine," Ethan said.

Nicholas widened his eyes, not expecting that response from his son. "You know what this means, don't you?" he asked. "You can't work for me anymore. No one will associate with you back at home. You'll be a nobody."

Ethan looked over at me, and where I expected to see fear or remorse, I instead saw confidence and calm. "I'll have the only person I need by my side." He held out his hand to me, allowing me the opportunity to make the choice and take it.

Did I want to? After everything he did this morning?

I did.

I slipped my hand in his, and it felt...right.

Nicholas's face turned beet red. "Fine! Have it that way." He turned to Rita. "By the way, pandas aren't endangered anymore."

Rita cackled a laugh. "You think I didn't know that? How stupid do you think I am? Of course I know they're not endangered anymore. But you took my daughter and grandson away from me. This benefit was the only opportunity I had to see them each year." She shook her head. "For someone so smart in business, you really have no clue."

Nicholas growled. Actually growled, like an animal. "Where is Rhonda?" he barked. "It's time to leave."

"I'm not coming with you," Rhonda said, slowly making

her way through the crowd that had formed around us. "I'm staying here. With my mother and Ethan."

Nicholas looked at her, fury in his eyes. "You know what this means," he said.

"Yes," she said in an unusually strong voice. "I won't be coming home, either."

Nicholas looked around the room, finally processing all the eyes on us. Without another word, he stormed out of the ballroom and didn't look back.

Stunned silence filled the ballroom.

Rita started clapping. "Oh, I've waited *years* for this!" She hugged Ethan around the waist. "Thank you, my boy, for being everything I hoped you would be." She took my free hand and squeezed it. "Welcome to the family, my dear. What a week you've had."

"Oh, um..." I stammered. "That's a bit premature, don't you think?"

She shook her head emphatically. "I see wedding bells for you two."

My eyes widened, and Ethan started coughing.

Once he cleared his throat, he leaned his head down to my ear. "Can we go talk somewhere in private?" he whispered.

"Yes, please," I said.

He squeezed my hand and led me out of the ballroom to the sound of Rita leading the guests in cheers and applause. We headed down the hallway and into a small, dark alcove.

"What is happ—" I started, but Ethan pushed me up against the wall and pressed his lips to mine.

All thoughts vanished. I couldn't think, only feel. His lips on mine. His hands on my waist. My hands on his chest, feeling the pounding of his heart.

The kisses went on and on, and I couldn't get enough. I could kiss this man forever.

His lips moved gently across my jawline, down my neck, and across my bare shoulder. He lifted his head to face me again, raising his hands to hold my face. "I am so, so sorry about this morning," he said, pressing another kiss to my lips.

"Which Ethan am I supposed to believe?" I murmured against his mouth. "Because present Ethan is very convincing."

He chuckled. "Present Ethan took his head out of his... you-know-what."

I smiled. "And this morning?"

"This morning was Ethan Flipping Taylor."

I pulled my head back, eyes wide. "How did you know about that nickname?"

He laughed out loud. "I've heard your conversations with Ivy. I know you call me that."

My cheeks flushed hot, and I was thankful that we were in the dark. "Well, it was true. Especially this morning."

"I was such an idiot," he said, leaning his forehead against mine. "You are literally a dream come true. And I pushed you away."

"But here we are now," I said. "What changed?"

He brushed his thumb on my cheekbone, carefully studying my eyes. "I spent some time with my mom and Gran this afternoon," he said.

"Your mom!" I said, remembering how she stood up to Nicholas. "What in the world was all of that about?"

His eyes turned sad, his fingers absentmindedly tracing up and down my arm, giving me shivers. "My parents have a lot more issues than I knew. And talking with Mom and Gran this afternoon made me realize how I don't want to be my father. I thought I needed to take his advice, follow his example, and be like him to get the status I wanted. But after talking to my mom and finding out just how miserable she's been...Did you know he's been cheating on her? Basically during their whole marriage?"

His wide eyes told me how shocked he was. "I'm not really surprised," I admitted. "But that's awful for your mom."

He sighed. "I guess I've been too naïve to see the truth behind their situation." He fixed me with a serious expression. "I have never cheated on anyone, and I never will. I can promise you that." He shook his head. "It's not like I wanted to be exactly like my dad. But I wanted his status and place in society. Which meant I took his advice seriously and still tried to impress him. But now, none of that matters." He pressed a gentle kiss to my cheek. "I love you, Thea. That's all that matters."

I blinked a few times. "Love?" I repeated.

"Yes," he said, kissing my lips. "I,"—*kiss*—"love,"—*kiss*— "you." Long, slow kiss.

I relaxed into him, letting him tell me without words how much he adored and cherished me.

I finally broke away from him. "We should get back," I said.

He shook his head, leaning in for another kiss. "No. Not yet."

"But your Gran," I protested.

He shook his head and kissed me again.

I pulled away. "Ethan," I said seriously. "The pandas need us."

He laughed out loud. "Well, how could I say no to that?" He kissed me one more time. "Come on, it's time to make a proper entrance."

$$Twenty\text{-}Five$$

ETHAN

Hand in hand, we walked back into the ballroom together. As we emerged through the entrance, Gran let out a loud cheer and started clapping, and all her guests followed suit. Thea blushed furiously, but I had to embrace the moment. I pulled her close to me and gave her a movie-style kiss (more chaste than the last ones, though, since we had an audience). The crowd went wild, and cheers and applause abounded.

The band started playing music, and Thea and I went to the dance floor.

"You dance, right?" she said.

"Haven't you seen me at other events?" I asked.

"Well, yeah. I couldn't help myself," she said with a smirk.

I loved flirty Thea. "Same here," I said to her. "And yes, I dance. Part of growing up with my mother included Cotillion, so I actually know quite a few formal dances, too."

"Oh, this is going to be fun," she said, a twinkle in her eye. "I've always hoped I'd be with someone who liked to dance."

"Perfect," I said, grabbing her hand and giving her a gentle twirl. She smiled from ear to ear, and I pulled her close to me, swaying to the music together.

I WISHED I could say I woke up feeling well-rested, but that was the opposite of true. Knowing that Thea was sleeping in the next room, just an adjoining door away, was torture. After kissing her and holding her tight, that's all I wanted to do. But no. She slept in her room, and I slept in mine.

I rolled over and looked at the clock. Six a.m. She would be awake by now, right?

I knocked on the adjoining door. "Are you up?" I called softly.

I waited a few painful moments, then the lock clicked, and the door creaked open. I was greeted by the most glorious sight. Thea, her red hair piled up on top of her head in a messy bun, and a pajama set of shorts and a tank top.

"Good morning to me," I murmured, reaching for her waist. She obliged and gave me a slow kiss.

"Good morning, handsome," she said. "Can't sleep?"

"Nope. Looks like you weren't able to, either."

She shook her head. "I'm glad you knocked, though."

"Want to go get some breakfast?" I asked. "Or coffee? Or walk?"

She laughed. "Sure. Let me get dressed."

I held on to her tighter. "Don't leave me yet."

"It'll just take a minute. You know I have my clothes strewn out all over my room."

"Don't remind me." I kissed her on the forehead. "Go get dressed."

Fifteen minutes later, we met in the hallway and walked hand in hand to the elevator. She was wearing another one of her flowy dresses, and I wore a simple button down and slacks.

"Do you ever wear a t-shirt?" she asked.

I made a disgusted face at her.

She laughed out loud. "I'll have to get you a Pokémon shirt. You can wear it around your house."

"That sounds awesome," I said. But I was already envisioning my home becoming *our* home. One day.

"What's the plan for today?" she asked.

"We have Carmen's show tonight, but not much else going on. Let's grab some coffee and head to the park."

She nodded and squeezed my hand. We got coffee at the shop down in the lobby, then took the hot and muggy walk to Central Park. It was mostly quiet this early in the morning, but we were happy to be together. We found a nice bench and sat, my arm around her shoulders and her body leaning against mine, sipping our drinks and watching the runners.

"Do you run?" she asked, breaking the silence.

I tilted my head back and forth. "Sometimes. I mostly lift weights."

"Yeah, I can tell," she murmured with a little giggle. I didn't think I could blush, but that was probably the closest I ever came to it.

"What about you? Do you run?"

She fixed me with a serious stare. "If I'm ever running, you should too."

"Why?"

"Because that means someone is chasing me."

I laughed out loud. "Really? You don't like to run?"

"Absolutely not. Worst form of exercise in the world. I will never again intentionally run for exercise."

I kissed the top of her head. "Well, you don't need to. Whatever you're doing is working for you."

Her cheeks burned red, and she buried her head into my shoulder. We settled into a comfortable silence. "So, I hate to change the subject like this, but...what's next?" she asked.

"What do you mean?"

"For you. You're obviously not going to work for your dad anymore. Do you have any idea what you want to do?"

I let out a sigh. The question was bound to come up, no matter how much I tried to push it away. "I don't know yet. I'm decent at my job, so I'm hoping another firm will take me on, even though I've clearly wrecked things with my dad." I shrugged. "We'll see. Right now, I just want to focus on the more important things."

She tilted her head up to me. "And what are those?"

"The fact that I have the perfect girl here in my arms, letting me hold her and kiss her." To prove my point, I leaned down and kissed her perfect lips.

She wasted no time in reciprocating, and before we knew it, we were tangled a little more than I would normally allow in public. But, hey, it was seven in the morning. We didn't have an audience or anything.

"Uh, this is *not* what I was expecting to walk up on," a familiar voice said from behind us.

Thea and I broke apart, startled. "Ivy?" she exclaimed.

I turned in my seat to see Lucas and Amy Carter, and Amy's best friend, Ivy.

And Ivy's fiancé.

Scott King.

What in the world was going on?

Thea jumped up and grabbed Ivy in a hug. "What are you doing here?"

"Stella Knight is performing tonight for Fashion Week," Lucas explained. "She offered to fly me and Amy out for the performance. Ivy figured out how to get an invitation for herself and Scott, too."

Stella Knight was the world's biggest pop/country star, and Lucas was one of her songwriters. And Ivy was... well, when Ivy wanted to make something happen, she would.

I was happy to see two of them. Amy and Lucas had become good friends of mine, two people I could count on who could see through my pretense. Just like Thea.

Ivy was fine. A little over the top, but I had been around worse. And Scott...well, everyone knew how I felt about him. I glared at him, but he gave me a nod. Of course he'd take the high road. So obnoxious.

"We flew in last night," Ivy added. "I remembered that your hotel was over here, so I convinced everyone to take a walk this direction. I was hoping to see you. But we didn't exactly expect to run into you two...like this." She waggled her eyebrows at Thea. "So I'm guessing everything is good now?"

Thea blushed even more than before. "Uh, yep. We're good now."

"Yes, we are," I said, giving Thea a squeeze and a kiss on the cheek.

"Finally!" Amy exclaimed. "Thank goodness you stopped being so gross."

I narrowed my eyes at her. "Thanks, Amy."

"No problem. Happy to call you out when you need it."

"Yeah, you can stop speaking your truth now."

Amy stuck her tongue out at me. The girls descended into chatter about the upcoming week, and I was happy to sit back and let Thea be in her own element.

Scott startled me by putting his hand on my shoulder. "Hey, can we talk privately?" he asked in a low voice.

What did he want? I glanced around at everyone, but they pretended not to notice the tension between us. "Sure," I said, standing up and following Scott over to a separate area. Amy and Ivy immediately took my place and I could hear them whispering all kinds of questions to Thea. Lucas looked a little uncomfortable, but he stayed back with the girls. I chuckled, grateful that Thea had some friends to share her life with. But mostly, I wanted her to share her life with me.

"I wanted to talk to you about what happened with your father last night," Scott said.

I raised an eyebrow at him. "I thought you guys didn't know what was going on here."

"I didn't say anything to the girls, because I wanted to confirm it first. Ron called me this morning."

That wasn't news. Ron was the associate at my father's firm. I didn't say anything.

"His cousin was at the benefit last night. He told me there

was a big falling out with your dad, and that he was extremely rude to Thea."

I nodded.

"And I heard that you've broken off your ties with him."

I nodded again.

He heaved a sigh. "I should have done the same myself, many years ago."

I raised my brow, surprised that would ever cross his mind. "What do you mean?" I asked.

"I've known that your dad isn't the most moral person," he said. "I never wanted to attach myself to him personally. But in business, I figured there was no harm that could be done. He took me under his wing and trained me, giving me opportunities that no one else would, and I thought I owed him my loyalty and respect." He paused for a moment, running a hand through his hair. "But what you did took integrity and courage. And I have to admire that."

I rubbed my chin. Dang it. Why was he doing the right thing? It was so much easier when I could imagine that he was a jerk and hate him.

"Thank you," I finally said.

He bobbed his head once in acknowledgment. "After I heard about last night, I've been doing some thinking. And I'm planning on resigning from the company."

"What? Really?" I asked.

"Yes. I think," he gestured over at Ivy, "you and I have the opportunity to make a new generation. To correct the wrongs of our parents. And that means taking a stand."

"And how do you plan on doing that?" I asked.

"By opening my own investment banking firm." He

looked me straight in the eye. "*Our* own investment banking firm. King Taylor Investing."

I raised my eyebrows. "You want to go into business with me?"

He nodded. "You're good at your job, even if you tend to play around more than you work. Your dad was too blinded to see it. I think we would work well together, as long as you got over whatever issues you have with me."

I chuckled. "I don't know about that."

"I think with your dad out of the picture, you'll see that I'm not such a bad guy."

I looked over at the girls and Lucas, who were watching us openly. Ivy waved at me. Maybe Thea was right. If Amy could forgive Scott, maybe there was something there, after all.

"I'll think about it," I said.

Scott grinned. "That's better than I expected." He slapped me on the shoulder and turned back to the girls.

Could I do it? Could I get over my rivalry with him?

We'd have to see how the next couple of days went.

I had to admit, King Taylor Investment Banking had a ring to it.

Twenty-Six

THEA

I watched Scott and Ethan with a little of trepidation. Ethan's arms were crossed over his chest for most of the time, and he didn't look like he was giving more than one-word answers to Scott, until Scott said something that changed his expression completely.

"What are they talking about?" I asked Ivy.

She shook her head. "I honestly don't know. Scott seemed like he really needed to talk to Ethan, but he wouldn't say what about."

We all watched them openly, and when Ethan looked over at us, Ivy waved.

"You're nuts," I said.

"But you love me," she said, squeezing me in a hug. "What the heck happened in the last day? Are you and Ethan together now?"

"Uh...yes," I said, fighting the blush that made its way onto my cheeks. I explained what happened after Ivy sent me the picture, how I kissed Ethan in his room, but he pushed me away.

"Are you kidding me?" she exclaimed. "I hope Scott punches him!"

"Ivy, chill out," Amy said. "If they're together, I'm sure there's some explanation we're missing."

"Thank you," I said to Amy, and launched into my explanation of what happened at the benefit.

"Whoa," Ivy said, her eyes wide. "I never thought I'd see the day that Ethan Taylor would sacrifice his reputation for someone."

Amy swatted her on the shoulder. "I knew he could. He just needed to see that it was worth it." She leaned around Ivy to smile at me. "I'm thrilled for you."

"Thank you," I said, looking over at Ethan and Scott. "I'm happy, too. But he has some things he needs to figure out."

Amy shook her head. "I'll help him through it. I've been there. He's going to be fine. If your actual family isn't there for you, friends become your family." Lucas squeezed her shoulder in solidarity, and Ivy gave her a hug.

I glanced back at Ethan and Scott again. He didn't have close friends, but maybe he would be willing to change that.

"His mom isn't as bad as I thought," I commented. "And his grandma is hilarious. I love her."

Amy laughed. "I haven't seen her in years. She was always a hoot."

Ethan and Scott were heading back in our direction, and while I was dying to find out what was going on, I didn't want to do it in front of everyone else.

We all made plans to get breakfast together and spend the day exploring. Even though they were all staying in a nearby hotel, the girls wanted to get ready with me before the show. I hadn't had girl friends like this since I moved up to Orange County, and I was getting a little tingle of excitement over getting ready with friends.

As everyone walked ahead of us, Ethan grabbed me around the waist and pulled me in tight. "I'm a little disappointed that I have to share you today," he said in a low voice, sending a shiver down my spine.

"Now I'm getting disappointed, too," I replied, drawing my face close to his.

"Don't make me steal you away."

"You'll have me all to yourself when we fly home." I kissed him gently. "What happened with Scott?"

He sighed, pulling his head back slightly but keeping our bodies close together. "He wants to open our own investment banking firm."

My eyes popped open. "You're kidding."

He shook his head. "I don't know if it's such a good idea."

I studied his expression, seeing the confused little boy who lost his father's guidance, and decided he needed a break. "Don't worry about it this second," I said, laying a gentle hand on his cheek. "You have an option, and that's enough. Let's enjoy today and worry about it when we get home."

"I like that plan," he said, a wicked grin lighting his face. "How about we just go back to the hotel and enjoy the day?"

"How about you calm yourself down?" I said with a laugh. "We've got a fashion show to attend."

THAT EVENING, our little group of six walked into Bryant Park for Carmen Valencia's fashion show. The giant white tents filled the space, and people milled all around.

"This is crazy," I breathed. "I can't believe I'm here."

Ethan tightened his grip on my waist. "You deserve to be here more than anyone I know."

"Thank you for bringing me," I said. "I feel like Cinderella at the ball."

His smile widened, and he kissed me hard. "You're adorable." He gestured inside the tent. "Let's go meet Carmen."

He pulled me by the hand and led me through the maze of people until we found Carmen Valencia. "Ethan! Thea!" she called out and waved us over.

"It is so good to meet you!" she said in a light Hispanic accent, squeezing me in a tight hug.

Was I in a dream? Over her shoulder, I mouthed *what is happening?!* to Ethan, who laughed.

"I can't believe I'm meeting you!" I said. "Thank you so much for this."

"Ethan would not stop talking about you," she said, giving him a wink. "He seems very smitten. I'm sorry that the media thought something was going on between us."

"It's all worked out now," I said, and Ethan protectively slid his hand around my waist again. "We've straightened everything out."

"Oh, you're too cute!" Carmen clapped her hands, then placed them over her heart. "This makes me so happy. Come, come. Let me show you around."

Carmen showed us around the entire tent, introducing me to models and other designers. I swore I had died and gone to heaven. It was literally a dream come true. We stopped at one more station, but no one was there.

"Who are we looking for?" I asked.

"Ah, Marcus!" Carmen called across the way. A tall, lanky man with glasses and shaggy blond hair gave Carmen a hug.

"Marcus Antonius," I whispered under my breath.

"You got this," Ethan whispered behind me.

I nodded, buoyed by his confidence in me.

"Marcus, this is my friend Thea. She's Ethan Taylor's girlfriend."

"Hello, Thea," he said, shaking my hand. "It's nice to meet you."

"Thank you. I love your designs," I said. Phew. At least my voice wasn't shaking, and I didn't totally fangirl over him.

"Thank you. Are you a designer yourself?"

I nodded eagerly. "Yes, I am. Hoping to make my way here one day."

He eyed me up and down carefully. "Did you design your outfit?"

I glanced down at the navy-blue crop top and high-waisted, wide leg gray trousers I had particularly planned for this evening. "Oh, this? Yeah, I did," I said as casually as I could.

"I like it," he said. "You have an eye for drape and color." He tapped his chin for a moment. "Do you have a portfolio?"

"Uh, yes." I pulled out my phone. "Here are a few of my sketches and some designs I've created."

I handed him my phone, and he scrolled through the pictures. Handing it back to me, he walked around me slowly, taking in every angle of the outfit I was wearing.

"Hey, now," Ethan warned.

I waved him off. "Hush, you. This is business."

He glared at Marcus but stopped complaining.

"Carmen, don't we have that event in Los Angeles next month?" he said.

Carmen nodded. "Yes, I had forgotten all about it." With Marcus still keeping his eyes on my clothes, Carmen gave me a sly wink.

"I want her on my team," he said, pointing at me.

My eyes widened. "What...what are we talking about here?"

His eyes snapped back up to mine. "We have a friendly little competition every year in Los Angeles. A few designers get together and make an outfit under constraints. Kind of like Project Runway, except we're already established design-ers." He laughed a moment, like it was so ridiculous to compare himself to the aspiring competitors of the show. "I want you on my team."

I looked back at Ethan, then Carmen, then back to Marcus. "Absolutely!" I exclaimed. "That sounds amazing."

Carmen sighed. "I was hoping I could have you on my team. But I suppose this works, as well."

"It's too late," Marcus said. "Thea already agreed. Have Carmen give you my number and we'll get in touch."

"That sounds great," I said. "Thank you!" He was already gone in another direction before I could give him a hug or kiss or do anything stupider than that.

Nothing was going to pull me down from this cloud. I was floating on air.

That was, until I saw Stefan and Tabitha.

Twenty-Seven

ETHAN

I saw the moment Thea spotted them. What were their names again? Stupid and Tasteless? No, that couldn't be right. But I didn't care enough to remember.

Tasteless was in a chair, getting her hair and makeup done, and Stupid was on his phone next to her.

"We can just go to our seats," I said to Thea. "They haven't seen you."

She straightened her spine. "Nope. We're going to go over there and rub it in their faces."

"Ooh, what's happening?" asked Carmen.

I gestured over at the pair. "That's Thea's ex-fiancé and his new girlfriend."

"Ah, I see." Carmen grinned. "How can I help?"

"Want to go make them jealous?" I asked.

"Absolutely!" Carmen clapped her hands.

Thea giggled behind her hand, and the three of us sauntered over to them.

"Hello, Tabitha," Thea said. "Stefan."

Oh, right. Those were their names.

"Thea!" Tabitha said, turning around in her chair. "I didn't expect to see you."

"I told you I'd be here," Thea said.

"Well, you know, sometimes you're all talk," Stefan replied.

Thea's eyes narrowed. I took a step forward to defend her, but she held a hand out to stop me.

"Let me introduce you to my friend. This is Carmen Valencia."

"Hello!" Carmen said with a friendly wave. "My friend Thea here is so amazingly talented. She's going to work with me and Marcus Antonius next month. I'm happy to meet friends of hers."

Thea interrupted. "Oh, no, Carmen. You've got it wrong. They're not friends at all."

Tabitha's jaw dropped, and Carmen covered her mouth in fake shock. "Oh, my mistake." I couldn't help the little chuckle that emerged.

"Well, great to see you all!" Thea said. Thea wrapped her arms around my waist and leaned her head on my chest.

"You're...really together?" Stefan asked.

I looked over at him curiously. "Why are you so surprised?"

"I, well," he stammered. "It just seemed like she was...I don't know."

"What did it seem like, Stefan?" Thea asked. She looked up at me, reconsidering, then back at him. "You know what? I don't want to know. But I have to thank you."

"Thank me?" he repeated.

"Yes. Thank you. Both of you. If we hadn't run into you that night, I don't know that things would have turned out this well." She looked back up at me, an adoring gaze I hadn't really seen before. I could have stayed lost there forever. "I don't know that I would have let love in."

I didn't care who was here, and who was watching. I cupped her face in my hands and kissed her with more passion and intensity than ever before. She melted in my grasp and returned the kiss.

"Woo-hoo!" Carmen called. "True love!"

Thea and I broke apart breathlessly, and her cheeks turned bright pink. She looked over at Stefan and Tabitha, gave them a simple nod, then grabbed my hand and pulled me away from them.

"Feisty Thea," I said to her. "I love it."

"I thought I was going to throw up," she said.

I laughed. "I knew you had it in you. The only girl who slapped me in the face can definitely stand up to people who knock her down."

She smirked.

"I like you two," Carmen said. "I can tell that next month is going to be fun." She glanced around the tent. "Well, I have to finish getting ready for the show. Have a wonderful night! Ethan, give Thea my number, as well."

"Will do. Thank you Carmen," I said.

"Thank you!" Thea added. Carmen waved and rushed off toward her station, and we were alone in the bustling crowd.

"Are you happy?" I asked Thea.

She nodded and went up on her tiptoes to kiss my lips. "Thank you, thank you, thank you."

"Did this change your mind about me?" I asked.

"What do you mean?"

"Are you still going to call me Ethan Flipping Taylor?"

She tilted her head. "Hmm, yes."

"Oh, really?" I asked.

"Yes. But more like, 'Man, I love Ethan Flipping Taylor.'"

My eyes widened. "Wait, what?"

She raised an eyebrow. "I didn't say I love you. Not yet. But maybe someday."

"Well, that's good," I said. "Because I love you, Thea."

Her perfect lips spread in a wide grin, and I couldn't help but kiss them. "You'll get there one day," I said with a wink.

I pulled her by the hand before she had a chance to respond. I didn't want her to feel pressure to say anything in return, especially because I had been harboring these feelings for her for over a year. She hadn't had the time to let it grow into love. And that was okay. We'd get there.

Epilogue

THEA

A year later, I kissed Ethan Taylor on the lips.

For the record, he deserved it.

Okay, okay, I had already kissed him many, *many* times that year. Even so, this time it was special.

We walked into the Cove Hotel, his arm around my waist.

"Carmen outdid herself with your dress," he commented.

"Right?" I looked down and smoothed the silky green fabric that fit my curves just right. "I'll have to tell her you liked it." I glanced around the hotel, assessing. "Which event are we here for tonight?"

"Oh, just another party," he said, continuing to lead me through the foyer. "Does it matter?"

I shrugged. "Guess not."

While I didn't *love* all the people at these events, I got used to being around them. And spending that week in New York with Ethan's family had opened my eyes to the struggles a lot of them were facing. Having that perspective allowed me to give them a bit of grace.

Ethan opened the door to the ballroom, and we found... no one. String lights were hung all around, and Dashboard Confessional's "Stolen" softly sounded through the speakers.

"What...where is everyone?"

"Hmm, that's strange," Ethan said with a wink.

Oh.

Oh shoot.

Was this...? Was he...?

"Do you remember what happened in this room about two years ago?" he asked.

I pretended to think, tapping my chin with my finger. "Hmm, remind me."

"Let me tell you a story," he said, guiding me around the room. "A very handsome man, adored by many, walked in through that door with someone else who is unimportant to this story." He pointed to a corner of the room. "Over there was a beautiful, stunning red-haired woman wearing an unfortunate uniform, but that's neither here nor there. The handsome man could see that, given the proper attire, she would be perfection."

I smacked him on the shoulder.

"Thank you for that reminder, because we're heading in that direction. The handsome man approached the beautiful woman, and very kindly asked if she would enjoy the pleasure of his company. No implications or innuendos, just a proper conversation between two extraordinarily beautiful people."

I raised my eyebrow at him. "That is a loose interpretation of reality."

He waved me off. "But she said no! Can you believe it? And not only that, she slapped him across the face."

I shrugged. "Sounds like he might have deserved it."

"Absolutely not. He had the best intentions. But she was deceived by outward appearances and didn't give him a chance."

"I'd like to think that the handsome man had some growing and changing to do as well."

"That's true." He stopped walking around the room and turned me to face him, wrapping both arms around my waist. "That man had to realize that the beautiful serving girl was the most precious thing in the world to him, and giving up everything was worth it to be with her." He kissed me on the forehead. "Thankfully, giving up everything meant starting his own company with his former nemesis and being extremely successful."

"True. That worked out well."

"He also realized," Ethan continued, lifting his hand to run his fingers through my hair, "that he needed to know more about the beautiful woman, beyond the fact that she was so beautiful. That he needed to support her goals and help her realize her dreams. With his help, she teamed up with some incredible designers and started her own fashion line."

I beamed. He was the best support I could've imagined, always so proud of me. Never in my wildest dreams did I imagine that self-centered Ethan Taylor could care so much about anyone else. But he did. He cared about me more than himself, and he showed me every day.

I buried my head in his chest, feeling his heart pounding

wildly. He was playing cool and collected, but I knew what was beneath the facade.

"And now, beautiful woman, this handsome man has a proposition for you."

I pulled my face away from his chest to look into his eyes. "I don't know if I want to be propositioned by you," I said, echoing the words I spoke to him a year ago.

He laughed. "I think you'll like this one. Because if you say yes, that means you'll spend every day, every night, every moment with the handsome man by your side." He reached into his pocket and got down on one knee. "Thea, you are the love of my life. You are perfect for me in every way. I promise I will always put you before myself. Will you be my wife?"

The stunning emerald-cut diamond sparkled in the case he held in his hands. But there was no need to decide or think about his question. I'd known, for a long time now, exactly where I was meant to be. "Yes," I said with a huge smile. "Yes, I'll marry you."

He jumped up, pulled me tight toward him and kissed me. "I love you, Thea," he murmured against my mouth.

"And I love you, Ethan Flipping Taylor."

He laughed and spun me around, and the doors to the ballroom burst open, people streaming in and cheering.

"What is this?" I asked, my eyes wide.

"It's our engagement party," he replied. I looked around the room and saw everyone special to us here: Amy and Lucas, along with their new little baby girl; Ivy and Scott, along with Ivy's family; students and parents from the dance studio; and last but not least, Rhonda Taylor and Rita.

Rita hobbled over to me first and squeezed me in a big hug. "Thea, my girl, welcome to the family," she said.

"I guess you were right after all," I said.

She laughed. "This old lady knew what she was talking about, even if no one else saw it."

I kissed her cheek. "Thank you for everything."

She patted my hand and hobbled away back to Rhonda, who was looking much healthier and happier these days. After moving back to New York, she quit the True Trophy Wives show and found a path to recovery that included divorce from Nicholas and a renewed relationship with her mother.

I sighed in happiness, taking in the crowd around us. I wished there were a couple more people here, though.

"Thea!" My mother's voice startled me. Did I imagine that?

I turned around and saw my mom and Miles behind me. Squeezing them into a big hug, I started to cry.

"No tears!" my mom exclaimed. "This is one of your special days. You deserve to be happy."

"I am happy," I said. "I'm so glad you're both here." Gathering myself, I wiped my eyes. "I wish Dad were here."

"Me, too," Mom said, cupping my cheek. "But I think we all know that he would have loved Ethan."

Ethan, who was giving Miles a fist bump and already planning their next StarCraft gaming session. He noticed my emotion and returned to my side. His steady hands held my waist, and he leaned in to kiss my cheek. "Everything okay?"

I turned around to look at him, wrapping my arms around his neck. "It is. Thank you for setting this up."

He leaned his forehead against mine. "Anything for you." He looked deep into my eyes. "I'm sorry it took me so long to get to this point."

"What do you mean?" I asked.

"It took me an entire year to show you how much better of a man I could be. And another year to get to the point of getting engaged. But I want you to know that I love you, with all my heart, and this is just the beginning of our journey."

"Don't worry," I said, kissing his lips once. "Perfection takes time."

And with a long, slow kiss, I knew the truth in those words. Because this was truly perfect.

THE END

Acknowledgments

I have so many people to thank. First of all, thank you to my amazing husband, who spent hours talking about my characters and plot and bringing the story to life. I cannot express how grateful I am for your support and encouragement.

Chelsea, you helped shape so many of the characters, too. I will never forget the hours we spent on the camping trip talking about Ethan's motivations and his parents. The story and characters are so much richer because of you!

My betas, you are the BEST!!! Christina, Laura, Tiarra, Malarie, Haley, and Whitney. You all gave me different perspectives but they meshed together and made this beautiful story.

Melody, I don't even have the right words to tell you how incredible your art is. Your illustrations and design for Ethan and Thea are PERFECTION. I'm so grateful for your friendship.

Jennifer, you're an incredible editor and proofreader. I'm so thankful I met you and that we have this relationship!

And finally, thank YOU, amazing reader, for taking the time to go on this journey with me. Being an author is still a dream come true! Thank you for making this dream a reality.

Canyon Cove Love Stories

Speak Your Truth

Feel the Rhythm

Let Love In

Take a Chance

Standalone Stories

Exceptional Emma

Love is a Roller Coaster

Once Upon a Rom-Com

Cookies & Kisses

Cinder Luna

Isabelle and the Beast

Lily of the Tower

Wendi & Peter

Marie has had two goals since she was seven years old: to be a mother, and to be an author. She has been a storyteller her whole life and loves sharing these stories with the world. When she's not writing, she can be found watching The Office, playing the piano, sewing a dress, or reading a book (while consuming copious amounts of chocolate). She lives in sunny Southern California with her husband of 16 years, four children, and their chickens.